TIMBUKTU

Granville Toogood

Just three months after graduation, I can't believe I'm already on a troop ship, off to fight with the American Expeditionary Forces in France. Thousands of cheering well-wishers pack every inch of Manhattan's West Side Pier, decorated with red, white, and blue bunting. Men wave hats, ladies blow kisses. Girls throw flowers. A band, heavy on the brass, plays "Over There" and a blizzard of confetti rains down.

But it's not exactly the kind of sendoff my father had in mind when I took my Princeton diploma, class of 1918.

"You'll have a solid place at the firm," he assures me. "And before long you'll have your own seat on the Exchange. Like me."

"Thanks, Dad," I tell him as he pumps my hand.

But what I don't tell him is that I don't want to be like him.

"Who'd have thought we'd be doing this?" my friend and Princeton classmate Harding Hapgood says, waving to the crowd as we pull away from the pier. We've been training in French Spads. In a few weeks we'll both be flying combat missions with the Air Service, U.S. Army, against German positions and German aircraft.

The ship's horn blasts.

"It beats Wall Street," I shout.

"Only if you come back alive," he says.

"You're gonna come back a hero."

He lights a cigarette and blows a plume of smoke into the wind.

"Never underestimate the Germans," he says. "Or their aeroplanes."

It's too late for us to take on the Red Baron, Manfried Von Richtofen, the great German Air Ace who only recently had bragged of his 80th kill as a fighter pilot.

The next day, he was dead.

Maybe it's a symptom. The war's been dragging on for four years. Americans are getting into the fight and there's talk the Germans are on their heels.

But with a little luck we're hoping to see action before they throw in the towel.

Besides the war, there's a lot going on.

The Spanish Flu has killed millions.

In Russia, Red revolutionaries executed the Tsar and his family.

Britain just launched the Royal Air Force. Maybe we'll get to go on missions with them.

Arriving in Amiens we share a flight barracks with two Belgian and two French pilots. One of the Belgians, Maurice Goesse, has already shot down two German Fokkers, both kills. But today's a special day, because yesterday Philippe, one of the French pilots, shot down another German, who crash landed just a mile from our headquarters. He walked away from the wreckage and tomorrow he's a guest of the people of France at a dinner in his honor. In Germany, they do the same. If you're a pilot and an officer and fall into German hands, they salute you as a fellow warrior and treat you with all the courtesy and respect due to a knight of the air.

Harding and I are assigned to bunks made vacant by the deaths of their occupants, two French pilots, a few days before. Over one of the bunks is nailed a tiny sepia photo of a pretty girl with hair piled on her head. She stares out at the observer with a look of uncertainty, as if she doesn't trust the camera to render her beautiful. But now it hardly matters, because the one who put her picture there is history.

"Looks like Eleanor," Harding muses.

"Your sister?"

"Yes. Don't you think?"

We decide to leave the picture on the wall in honor of Eleanor, and to remind us of home and what we're fighting for. But the truth is, we're really fighting for ourselves.

"We're not fighting for Eleanor," I suggest to Harding the next morning when I see him staring at the little picture. "We're fighting for glory, for adventure, because we want to be aces. And so do the Germans. And that's why we're honoring a German prisoner of war tonight, because we're honoring ourselves. We're all part of the same brotherhood of warriors."

"He could be the fellow who shot down the fellow who slept in this bed last week," Harding says.

"Or this bed. The German guy's bed is going to be empty too for a while. But at least he's still alive."

Our first missions begin in two days. According to our squadron leader, a thirty-three-year-old French veteran they call the Le Vielle Homme, the Old Man. The survival rate among pilots on both sides is currently running at about 20 percent. Which means we're more likely than not to get shot down every time we go up.

"If I'd known the odds, I wouldn't have signed up for this," Harding says bleakly.

"Think about Eleanor. And while you're at it, grab your field jacket. The officer's mess is in five minutes."

Pilots from other squadrons are pressing against the crowded bar, calling for drinks. The tallest, a mustachioed gent I'm told is a French count, pops the cork to a bottle of champagne and pours half of it into his mouth. The rest he splashes around into upraised glasses. The Count then leads the assembled crowd into a rousing rendition of the "Marseilles." The entire room explodes into a patriotic salute at the coda, all glasses held high. Someone pops a second bottle, someone else a third, and before long, Harding and I are tossing back one glass of champagne after another.

"Vive La France!" booms the Count. "Vive La France!" everybody echoes.

One of the pilots sits down at the piano and starts to play.

"Eat, drink and be merry, my friend," Harding shouts over the din, "For tomorrow we die."

The windows are drawn with black curtains to hide interior lights from spying German eyes. Germans could be just across the field in the woods, or overhead in reconnaissance balloons running silent in the night. The Spads, crouching on the ground like frogs ready to leap into a pond, are hung with camouflage nets.

The door bangs open and a senior French officer walks in escorting the German pilot, dressed in full flight gear: black jacket, black trousers, black boots.

"This must be our man," Harding says.

The room goes silent.

"Gentlemen, I would like to present Captain Heinrich Von Sachs Und Brachen, of the Fliegertruppe, air arm of the German Army," the French officer announces in English.

The German snaps to attention and salutes. We all return his salute.

"And now, gentlemen, may we ask you to join us?" the French officer says. The entire bar follows him and the German prisoner down a short corridor to the mess hall, where we take our places at a long dinner table. Not twenty minutes later a door opens and a courier walks over to the commanding officer, whispers something and places a dispatch in his hands. The room goes completely silent while the commander reads. After a moment, he raises his eyes, comes to his feet, and announces with grave solemnity: "Gentlemen…the war is over! Germany has surrendered!"

No one moves. You can hear a butterfly dance.

"Dodged a bullet!" Harding mutters under his breath.

Every man rises as one and the Marseillaise bursts forth in a deafening chorus. Captain Sachs Und Brachen is the last on his feet, ramrod straight, mouth clenched, but he snaps a fine salute.

When the anthem concludes, the Count shouts, "More Champagne! Champagne!" Within seconds, orderlies appear and begin placing extra champagne bottles all around the table. Empty bottles disappear, replaced by full ones. The popping of corks sounds like artillery, and air is thick with blue cigarette smoke. By the time dinner is finally over, even Captain Von Sachs Und Brachen is toasting the end of the war and joining in for a final rendition of the French national Anthem.

"We never even got in a single mission," I grouse.

"You disappointed?"

"Damn right. I'll never know what I missed."

"What you missed is being a grease spot on some farmer's field in France."

After the squadron disbands, Harding talks about getting a flying job back home. He takes a train to Brest, and a troop ship bound for New York. Unlike Harding, I'm not prepared to go back to the States and the boring job I know awaits me on Wall Street.

The end of the war puts an end to any fanciful thoughts of a military career. But it kick-starts my new life as a jewel thief, a curious situation I never could have imagined back at Princeton.

2

I first hear about Baron Jacques de Sehrgitz, a Belgian arms merchant and former calvary officer with longstanding ties to German business interests, while still training with my squadron in Amiens, at the very the end of the war.

"He's a collaborator, a traitor! A spy! A cochon! A real pig!" Maurice Goesse had fumed one night over a round of beers in the mess. "His brother-in-law is Prussian. The bastard trades diamonds from the Germans in exchange for information. The family has good connections. I have it on good authority that Sehrgitz arranges for anonymous parcel packages containing the diamonds to be stored for safe keeping in the Belgian Embassy in Paris. Hides them right under everybody's noses in a common wall vault. Very clever. It's the last place you'd expect to find stolen goods, yes? If I survive, I'm going to track him down."

"You think you might need a little help?"

"Why do you ask?"

"I'm not ready for Wall Street."

"Then we'll liberate those diamonds. I mean a lot of diamonds! What do you think?"

"I think it's worth a try. I assume you are talking about returning the diamonds to their rightful owners?"

"There are no rightful owners."

"What about helping all the people whose lives were ruined in the war? What about the families of wounded and dead soldiers? What about them?"

"But of course, mon ami! We would never forget them! But I assure you, there are reportedly plenty of diamonds to go around. And while we're at it," he says, giving me a sly look, "Maybe we can also do something for ourselves! Why not?"

"You mean, steal diamonds? Wouldn't that make us jewel thieves?"

"Stealing jewels from a jewel thief does not mean you are a thief."

"What *does* it mean, then?" I really have to think about that.

"It simply means you're immune from guilt," Maurice responds dismissively. "Besides, it's only fair that we compensate ourselves for our trouble."

What comes over me at that moment? Could be the temptation of the forbidden? An exotic notion of undreamed-of adventure? Or just a nice buzz from the beer? Suddenly I'm overwhelmed with a boyish flush of reckless abandon that washes away all presumption of guilt.

"Then here's to a life of crime for the common good!" I burst out laughing, clicking my glass to his.

"To Robin Hood and the common good!"

"To Robin hood!"

3

The ball at the Belgian embassy in Paris to celebrate the end of the war is in full glittering swing when Maurice and I arrive in our Air Service uniforms. I cut a pretty good figure, and speak a little French, so no one questions me at the door. I just walk in with other uniformed guests and take a glass of excellent champagne from a silver tray. The great hall is hung with a dozen candlelit chandeliers and a string orchestra plays. Diplomats wearing colorful sashes and tails dance to waltzes with some of the most beautiful women I've ever seen. A few wear tiaras. You'd never know the world had just fought the greatest war in history.

I'm working my way around the perimeter of the dance floor when I feel a hand on my elbow.

"I've been upstairs, looking for the wall safe," Maurice tells me excitedly. "I found it behind a panel in the library. I don't know the combination, but a friend tells me he has it on good authority that Sehrgitz may be planning to make off with the diamonds tonight. With all the activity, he would hardly be noticed. It's his best chance. He has enough friends and influence that he'll feel safe. That's exactly how we want him to feel. He has no idea."

"How do you know the diamonds are still here?"

"I don't. Nobody does. But my friend may be right. He usually is. We'll just have to wait and see."

It's almost midnight when we're ready to give up that I hear Maurice say:

"That's him! The one with the monocle."

The man coming down the steps, wearing the Prussian-style monocle, also sports a Van Dyke beard and full-dress cavalry officer's uniform. He's already caught the attention of a large woman in a green satin gown, and an elderly man in an old-style military uniform. They both greet him warmly.

"The old one," Maurice says. "That's the ambassador. You can see for yourself Sehrgitz has friends in high places."

Then he turns to me. "Sure you're still in?"

"I'm in." I don't hesitate.

"Good. Now, it's up to Sehrgitz. Stay with me. Check your piece. If he makes his move, we'll follow."

Sehrgitz mills about in the crowd and moves slowly towards the rear of the room, finally disappearing through a service door.

We shadow him up the rear stairs and proceed down a long corridor, stopping to listen at the library entrance.

Maurice turns to me and nods. We step together into the room, pistols in hand.

Sehrgitz, busy opening the safe, is unaware of our presence.

"You can hand over those diamonds, Monsieur Sehrgitz," Maurice says.

Sehrgitz spins and stares at us with a look of astonishment.

"Who are you?" he asks.

"Never mind. Hand over the diamonds."

Sehrgitz glances at each of us, assessing the situation.

"Gentlemen," he says, in a calm voice. "Let us be reasonable. There's a great deal more where these came from. Riches beyond your imagination. I'm sure we can work out an accommodation that would be agreeable to both of you."

"We don't do business with traitors," Maurice says. "Hand over the diamonds."

After a long moment, Sehrgitz says, "Of course…" He turns, reaches into the open safe, wheels around with a gun and fires a shot. Maurice steps back, gripping his shoulder. Sehrgitz turns the gun on me and fires a second shot just as I'm firing at him. Sehrgitz stares at me in disbelief, drops the gun and falls over backwards, leaving the room filled with silence and the smell of cordite.

"Are you alright?" I turn to Maurice.

He pulls his hand from his shoulder and stares at the blood on his fingers.

"It's nothing. Is the bastard dead?"

Sehrgitz appears to be gaping at the ceiling in a state of shock, but his eyes are already glazing over. I can see the little black hole in his chest surrounded by a blossom of red.

I put my hand to his neck. No pulse.

"I think he's dead."

Maurice rushes to the open safe and pulls out a leather handbag. He opens the bag, looks inside, closes it, tosses it to me, then shuts the safe. He stoops over the body and with a handkerchief places the gun back in Sehrgitz's hand, then rests the hand holding the gun on Sehrgitz's chest.

"Come on!" he says, making for the library entrance. "Let's get out of here before somebody discovers there's a dead body in the embassy."

We take the rear stairs and slip out the back without incident. On the street, we keep going until we reach a park and find a bench.

"How's the shoulder?" I ask, handing him the bag.

"I'll see to it later," he says, walking to a pool of light beneath a streetlamp, opening the bag and peering inside.

"Diamonds! Diamonds! Hundreds of diamonds!" he says, barely able to keep his voice down.

He steps back into the shadows and joins me on the bench.

"It's a fortune," he says. "So now we have other things to consider. To begin with, we have a dead body. Will it look like a suicide? I don't know. The story is likely to appear in the newspapers. Since we can't be certain that we escaped altogether undetected, we should make ourselves scarce. I'm particularly concerned about you, as a foreigner. You probably saved my life, but you happened to fire the fatal shot. In a court of law it could become complicated, and we must make certain it never gets that far. Even a manslaughter conviction can put a man in jail for years. But I'm certain the guilt would fall to both of us in a jury trial."

His words shake a little reality into me.

I never get to fire a single shot in the war, and it has never crossed my mind to kill anyone outside of combat --even in self-defense. Now what started as a mere caper has in seconds ballooned into a capital crime with potentially profound consequences. I'm still in shock, wrestling with the reality that I've just killed a man and stolen diamonds.

But there's also a little thrill of accomplishment and excitement.

"I have a friend who can put us up for a few days until things blow over," Maurice is saying. "Sehrgitz is controversial. It may be that the incident will simply quietly be forgotten, and we have nothing to fear. But for good measure, you must vacate your hotel at once, leaving a forwarding address that puts you somewhere in Australia or the Far East."

My heart is racing.

"The second issue is, where are the remaining diamonds?" he continues. "I have no doubt Sehrgitz was telling the truth. My friend tells me Sehrgitz has been in collaboration with the Germans for years, and it only makes sense that he would not stash all the loot in the same place. I intend to recover the remaining diamonds, however difficult that may be. You in for that?"

Do I still have a choice?

By the time we arrive at Maurice's safe house, just outside the city, morning sun is already filtering through the trees. The meadow smells fresh, and a light fog rises as the grass warms. A small, spectacled man in a worn wool sweater steps outside to greet us. Several sheep are clustered on the far side of a low hedge.

"Max, this is Gaston, my friend."

We shake hands. Gaston ushers us into the warm kitchen, where we seat ourselves on wooden chairs.

"What happened?" Gaston asks in French, pointing to Maurice's shoulder. "Let me have a look," He pulls a box off a shelf, opens it, and begins to tend to the wound.

"Excellent. Very clean. Just a grazing," Gaston observes as he applies iodine, stitches the wound, and puts on a bandage. "I did dozens of these during the war, and worse."

Maurice tells Gaston, gesturing in my direction: "This man has my complete confidence. He's with me."

An older woman putters in the kitchen, stirring pots and muttering to herself. In minutes, we're sharing a pot of fresh black coffee.

"Delicious," I tell Gaston. "My compliments. Good coffee is very hard to come by."

"Courtesy of the retreating German Imperial Army," Gaston chuckles. "We liberated their entire supply."

Later, over a bottle of local red, Maurice tells Gaston about the events of the Embassy evening. I can't determine if Gaston works for Maurice, or

Maurice works for Gaston. Or whether they operate independently. I don't ask.

One thing, however, is clear. Gaston does not appear to operate alone and has information of vital interest to Maurice.

"One of my associates tells me that he's traced the missing diamonds to a smuggling syndicate that operates out of Africa," Gaston says. "The Germans were familiar with Sehrgitz's love of gems and exploited his greed. The war was a business opportunity that he couldn't resist."

Gaston throws another log on the fire.

Maurice stares into the erupting sparks and leaping flames, shaking his head.

"Incredible," he says. "Just incredible. The bastard betrayed his country for a small pile of rocks. What kind of a man is that?"

When it comes to diamonds, I can't help wondering if Maurice might be such a man.

"A dead man, apparently," Gaston says, looking at me with a little grin.

"This is blood money," Maurice persists. "I'm going to do something about it."

"Let me know what you want to do, and maybe I can provide some assistance," Gaston says, rising from his chair and heading toward the door. "But right now I have to go tend to the sheep."

When he's gone, Maurice turns to me. "What do you think?"

"About what?"

"About your future. What are you going to do?"

"There's a lot to think about. What happens with those diamonds you just gave Gaston?"

"Gaston's like a brother. He's one of us. There's plenty to go around. I'll sit down with him later. We get ours. He gets his. The rest goes to the victims of Sehrgitz's treachery, to families of soldiers killed as a result of military secrets he supplied the Germans, and families of the underground operatives who were betrayed and executed, and the survivors of villages and towns destroyed out of spite--like we said."

Not quite.

"But you believe this is only part of his loot. Where's the rest?"

"That's what I intend to find out."

"Well, you can count me in."

"You need to think about this. This isn't your fight."

"But it is now. I'm the one who killed Sehrgitz. Now I'm an accomplice."

"It will probably blow over. Then you can relax, maybe go back to the States. Have a normal life."

Maurice is hard to read.

Does he want me to come with him or not?

"But maybe it won't blow over," I tell him. "And you're right, if it all goes wrong we could both end up in a French jail. Not to mention the headlines. Besides, I've got nothing to go home to."

He looks at me.

"Well, if you're in, it could take you to Africa."

"Well, then, let's go to Africa."

From the window, I can see Gaston walking among the sheep.

"Who is Gaston?" I ask Maurice.

"It's better that you don't ask."

"It would be helpful to know who he is, since it looks like I'm going to be a part of this thing."

"If you were to know, it would only put you in peril. Gaston has many friends. But he also has many enemies. It's enough that I know him. That's really all you need to know."

"Is Gaston even his real name?"

"No."

"If he's dangerous, why do you do business with him?"

"Because it's more dangerous not to. In the world we live in, danger is the norm. I trust him. If I have a problem, Gaston can help me. If it were not for him, we would not know about Sehrgitz and the diamonds."

Outside, Gaston picks up a baby sheep, cradling it in his arms.

"And what about you, Maurice? Who are you?"

Maurice grins wryly. "I like to think of myself as a patriot...After all, I shot down Germans. But let's be frank. I'm a patriot who's not afraid to seize an opportunity."

"Such as missing diamonds?"

"Precisely."

"You mean for yourself..."

"I mean for you, too...What do you think of that?"

"This is your show, Maurice. I'm just along for the ride."

"I'm making you an offer, Max," he says. "We're talking about a lot of money."

"Why would you want to cut me in?"

"Because I'm going to need help. And we're talking about more riches than you can imagine. There's plenty to go around."

"What about all this talk to repatriate the diamonds?"

He looks away, then asks me:

"What about you?"

"I like to think I'm a patriot. But I came here to fly airplanes. Maybe I'm a soldier of fortune and don't even know it."

"Now maybe you do. You'll never have an opportunity like this as long as you live."

That evening, we dine on roast baby lamb with fines herbs and a fine local cabernet. I suspect the lamb is the same little creature I had seen in Gaston's arms. Eating with slow deliberation and sipping his wine discreetly, Gaston begins talking.

"With Sehrgitz dead, it may be difficult to trace the remaining diamonds," he cautions us. "But we have good intelligence as to where the Germans sourced their diamonds. The diamonds originate in Congo or Angola. But the key to the money distribution process is almost beyond grasping. There are multinational players in the consortium. Sehrgitz may have been a member of the consortium himself. He may be a traitor, but who knows? The principal player would appear to be a man known simply as El

Gato, scion of an old Spanish family, who is believed to be living in Spanish Sahara. He has agents who manage the diamond trafficking. He's omnipotently powerful, super-secret, and famously elusive. Everyone's in awe of him and scared into obedience.

"Meanwhile, the syndicate has not escaped the attention of a number of legitimate and rogue government interests, who are reported to be actively in pursuit of El Gato themselves. So he's under pressure. But that makes our mission even harder. The first task is to find El Gato. That's the key to access the illicit diamond trade."

We eat in silence for a moment, as Gaston pauses.

"If you're serious in your wish to continue your quest for the diamonds, you must understand that the odds are overwhelmingly against you. The particular diamonds you seek may be hidden here in Europe. But with Sehrgitz dead, it's impossible to know, and their whereabouts has escaped our intelligence."

While I find myself thinking about the little sacrificial lamb, Gaston's clearly relishing the delicious, juicy meat.

"In Africa, if your presence becomes known, you'll have to be very careful not to be seen as opportunistic meddlers," he goes on. "Your lives will depend on it. You may pose a threat to everyone within the consortium, both the good guys and the bad guys, so there could be an immediate effort to have you disappear."

24

I glance at Maurice.

I can't read him.

"But there's a way," Gaston continues, "that might prove to be a good start. We know that the key north African distribution agent is a man by the name of Mustapha Aziz, who goes by the name of Fasi. He lives in Marrakesh with an office in Casablanca and is believed to be the gatekeeper for syndicate diamonds bound for European markets. We will arrange for a meeting, and you can position yourselves as investors, or perhaps buyers. We will provide letters of introduction and suitable passports to disguise your true identities."

I can hardly believe what I'm hearing. Suddenly Princeton seems like a child's fairy tale. Maybe Maurice is right. Maybe this isn't my fight. But then why am I allowing myself to be sucked into the flame?

Maurice rises from the table, walks to the window and gazes up, perhaps looking for stars. Gaston addresses him directly.

"Maurice, are you listening?"

After a long moment, Maurice turns and says, "When can we begin?"

4

Things don't go as planned. As an American, I require additional briefing, more documentation, intense counseling. I'm considered a heightened risk, and Maurice advises me that I might have to go home and take that job on Wall Street after all. Our departure is delayed, then delayed again. But in the end, Maurice and Gaston manage to produce a nicely crafted new identity and some very authentic-looking forged documentation to go with it. There follow several weeks of intense training to indoctrinate me in my new identity coupled with a crash course on the ins and outs of the legitimate – and illegitimate – diamond trade.

I've developed such an addiction to adventure for adventure's sake that it doesn't properly cross my mind that I might be breaking international law.

One day, Maurice asks: "What did they teach you about hand-to-hand combat in the Lafayette Escadrille?"

"Not much. Target practice with a pistol."

"Seems to have paid off with Sehrgitz. But where we're going, you'll also need to learn close combat."

"Close combat?"

"You have to learn to kill."

"I already seem to have a talent for that."

"There's a lot about killing you don't know."

"Why is that necessary?"

"Africa's dangerous. It's not the animals. It's the people. If something happens, I want to know you can handle yourself. We need to have each other's backs."

I discover immediately the price that must be paid to become a reliable companion in the unforgiving and treacherous Sahara. Andre Chirac, a grizzled Belgian Corps commander, former Foreign Legionnaire, and old Africa hand with a unique talent for inflicting pain, becomes my constant companion for the next four weeks and introduces me to a level of misery I never thought I'd have any reason to endure, let alone master.

But it never occurs to me to quit.

I suffer a bloodied nose, loose tooth, lacerations, contusions.

Andre teaches me the hard way how to deflect a gun at my chest, disarm the assailant and kill him with his own weapon.

"Encore!" he shouts every time I get it wrong, knocking me to the ground.

I learn how to parry a knife and kill the attacker with just two moves.

"Non!" he yells, swatting me sideways.

"Comme ca!" he shouts again, nearly breaking my arm.

I learn how to incapacitate a man with just my forefinger, how to kill him with two fingers.

"Tu es un idiot!" he bellows, over and over, thrashing me aside each time I try unsuccessfully to penetrate his defenses.

I learn how to debilitate two attackers simultaneously. But the price is high, a broken rib and black eye.

"Kill me!" he bellows. "Come on! Kill me!"

It's not until I actually try to kill him that he gives me a pat on the back and tells me I'm almost there.

After twenty hours of target practice, I can hit the bullseye every time, rapid-fire, double grip. It's only when I never miss that he smiles for the first time and finally tells me that I'm ready.

Meantime, he's instructing me in the fundamentals of wilderness survival. I'll be issued a first aid kit, knife, water purification tablets, anti-venom, compass, scarf (for sandstorms), fire starter. I learn how to find water beneath the beds of wadis and dry lake beds and near the base of mountains; to avoid eating if there's no water; to travel at night whenever possible and use my urine to dampen my clothes and preserve perspiration. He tells me that if I'm lucky enough to spot a bee, follow the bee. Bees fly in a straight line to and from water.

He shows me how to grub out edible roots, cactus, and insects for food and moisture.

"The big ones, the white grubs, are full of fat and calories," he tells me. "You can live for days on a just a handful of them. They are delicious roasted over a fire, but I also like to eat them raw. Like oysters."

Maurice, he says, is an experienced desert hunter who knows how to find and harvest the larger wild critters of the desert, including desert hare, wild boar, snakes, and the occasional armadillo.

"I never could eat the snakes without wanting to puke," Andre acknowledges in a rare admission of human weakness. "But underneath all those scales, armadillo is pretty tasty, if you can find one."

I've never felt so alienated from my roots, nor so distantly removed from the hallowed halls, ivied walls, eating clubs, and time-honored playing fields of Princeton. It's an even further cry from the glamorous and chivalric notion of flying around the sky in Spads.

Just ten days into the course, Maurice announces that circumstances require him to leave for Malta without delay, with plans to reunite on a certain date at the Mamounia Hotel in Marrakesh, Morocco.

So I'm on my own.

5

When I finally disembark from a passenger liner in Casablanca several weeks later, I set out on foot to find the offices of the mysterious merchant, eventually locating him in an elegant apartment over a shop in the casbah that sells brassware hand-fashioned by a small army of young boys, and one old man with a flowing white beard who looks like Moses.

Upstairs, I step into a bizarre world, greeted by a large and effeminate man, clad in full Arabian regalia and colorful silks, spangled in gold baubles. He salaams several times and ushers me ceremoniously into plush rooms where I'm greeted by a rotund fellow with a florid face wearing an embroidered kaftan and scarlet fez.

"Mr. Kilgalen, I presume?" the man says, rising to shake my hand. He sports a waxed handlebar mustache and gold rings on the fingers of both hands.

"You must be Mustapha."

"The very same," he says, gesturing for me to take a seat on a raft of cushions. "Let us indulge ourselves in the best sweet mint tea in all Casablanca."

He snaps his fingers and the tall turbaned gent I take to be a eunuch produces crystal goblets on a silver tray and begins to pour tea. I notice a gold earring dangles from the lobe of one ear.

"You may call me Fasi," the merchant says, settling back on the cushions.

Before I can even get my first sip, he starts his interrogation.

"Tell me, have you ever been to Morocco?"

"No. This is my first visit."

"Then you're not familiar with the sirocco winds?"

"Never heard of them."

"The siroccos blow in from the Sahara and continue for days," he explains. "They cover everything with sand. There's no escape. Even the furniture is covered with dust. They're so relentless that Moroccan men who wish to escape prosecution wait every year until the siroccos to murder their wives, claiming insanity. It works every time. We're expecting those winds to come any day now, so the whole country is bracing for a new wave of murders. Of course, if wives kill their husbands, the same defense does not apply. So the mortality rate in the wind season is always measured in female lives. What does a Westerner such as yourself think of that?"

"Do you want me to make a moral or cultural judgement?"

"As you wish."

"Then I'll tell you I think it's inarguably wrong morally, but merely incomprehensible and unknowable culturally."

"That's an interesting observation," Fasi says, giving me an assessing look.

"You're fortunate to have escaped the war, Fasi," I say, moving on.

"Ah, but I did *not* escape," he counters. "Nobody escaped. European powers are already carving up the Levant and most of the rest of the Arab world to serve their own ends, creating a crazy quilt cartography of straight lines that cut across tribal, ethnic, and cultural territories. The Middle East has been totally redrawn. Nothing can ever be the same. And here in North Africa, Colonial interests dominate. But Morocco has managed to escape the worst of it, in spite of the French. In fact, I rather like the French. They've been good to me. As have the Germans, the British and also the Spanish."

"What has been the source of all this personal good fortune, if I may ask?"

"Perhaps you yourself might be part of the answer."

"I don't understand."

"Surely you understand why you're here?"

"Please enlighten me."

"Very well. I'm told you've come to Africa to position yourself as an interested party wishing to engage in the diamond trade. But you're really a soldier of fortune on a mission to find Baron Sehrgitz's lost diamonds. Am I right?"

"Go on."

"I know all about you. So we can dispense with the hide-and-seek. To be clear, we're on the same side. We're both in search of the same treasure. Yes, I'm a diamond merchant and a businessman with, you might say, useful connections. But I'm also an opportunist with an exceptional talent and capacity for flexibility, which is the reason I've survived so long in such a dangerous line of work."

Fasi's eyes darken. The friendly smile is gone.

"You can think of me as your home base in Africa, the contact for all future transactions," he says. "So you may continue in your adopted role without interference. However, to be candid, we have a special need of the services of someone unknown, an outsider with special skills, to put it delicately."

"Special skills?"

"Former military, like you. And at least one successful assassination to your credit. The kind of man we can rely upon to take care of himself without attracting too much attention and able to make his way quietly through difficult situations. Someone who, from time to time, might be able to perform an important service for us."

"Such as?"

"I believe you understand what I'm driving at."

"I've never assassinated anybody in my life."

"Perhaps you're forgetting the recent misfortune that befell Baron Sehrgitz?"

"Self-defense," I say flatly. "He was trying to kill me."

"But he didn't. You're sitting here and he's not. Isn't that the point?"

"Did you know him?"

"Only too well. We discovered he'd been stealing from the consortium," Fasi says. "His days were numbered. But you saved us the trouble. The man's greed knew no bounds. He wasn't content with the German bribes. He had to have more. I'm in a business driven by greed. But I've never seen anything to compare to Sehrgitz."

"How much is missing?"

"Diamonds in the magnitude of fifty million dollars, US currency."

The sum gives me pause.

"That's a lot of money. What do you want of me?"

"I want what you want, of course," Fasi says. "The consortium wants to find the lost diamonds. That's what you want, isn't it?"

He pauses to take another sip of his tea.

"I don't know where to begin," I confess. "I was hoping you might have some ideas."

"As a matter of fact, I do," Fasi says. "Everything traces back to El Gato. El Gato controls everything. But he's notoriously secretive. I, for one, have never laid eyes on him. No one in the consortium has any idea what he looks like or where he lives, though he's known to have residences in Europe and Africa. His real name is Emilio Carrado Sanchez de Narhona, born to an aristocratic family in Cadiz, but spent much of his youth in Spanish Sahara, which is no more than a family fiefdom. He's one of the richest men in the world."

It's beginning to sound to me like a fool's errand. A dangerous fool's errand.

"Sounds hopeless, like trying to find a ghost," I tell Fasi.

"True. It might sound that way because there's no reliable way to track him. But the best way is to begin with the diamonds, and the diamonds begin at Fucauma in the Angolan mines of Ama, the most productive in the world. They are under the protection of Katana, king of the province of Luena, who calls himself Sultan of Cumara. El Gato's family has a long relationship with Katana. The consortium pays an exorbitant sum every year for exclusive access. El Gato makes several visits annually to Fucauma, where he's always a guest of Katana in the Sultan's palace. That's a good place to start.

"Alternatively, because of its remoteness, we keep a trading post on the far side of the Atlas massif, a place consigned to only the most sensitive transactions. Two weeks ago we heard from one of our people in Meknes that El Gato was expected there before the end of the month to arrange for a private shipment of diamonds to Tsar Nicholas of Russia. But the Tsar and his family are now dead, so I don't know what's become of those diamonds or if El Gato even showed up."

"And suppose I manage to track him down?" I ask. "What makes you think he'll know where the missing diamonds are?"

"If he doesn't know, no one knows. He was the only contact for the Baron. All transactions went through El Gato."

"Is it possible that El Gato himself is part of the problem?"

"Like the Mafia, El Gato is Don of the family enterprise. But he's supervised and closely monitored by the Council, a secret family institution going back hundreds of years. They control a fortune larger than the capital wealth of many nations. Any family member who steals from family interests is quickly dealt with. Even if he were to be tempted, El Gato fully understands the consequences."

"What about people who steal from him?"

"Many have tried. None has survived."

I have to think about that. But I ask:

"What else should I know about this ghost?"

"I can tell you all you need to know about your ghost!"

Powdered with sand and dust, Maurice strides unannounced into the room, fresh off the desert. He greets us and takes a seat on a cushion as the eunuch steps up to pour mint tea. Fasi, speaking in Arabic, returns the greeting.

"Where have you been?" I ask, astonished. "You're covered with dirt."

He laughs at me.

"That's something you have to get used to if you're going to spend time in Africa."

"I thought you were in Malta."

"I was. But in this business things don't always go as planned."

Fasi nods knowingly. "What happened to you?"

"Greed happened. I had to beat a hasty retreat. The meeting was arranged by a third party. I showed up with a trusted associate and walked straight into an ambush. The only business they were interested in was robbing us."

"And then what?"

"Well, fortunately, my associate and I were faster and better than in the recent skirmish with Baron Sehrgitz in Paris." Maurice gives me a nod of appreciation. "That was the only shootout I ever lost – in fact the only one in which I ever took a bullet. Just now, in Malta, when the smoke cleared, we were the only ones standing. We were at sea in a fast boat ten minutes later on our way to Morocco."

"Just another day at the office."

"You could say that. But close calls are never funny."

"So this is the kind of thing I can expect?"

Maurice and Fasi exchange glances.

"You can expect only the unexpected," Fasi says. "That's the key to good health and a long life."

"It's not too late to opt out," Maurice says, testing me.

"I'm in the game to play. But sometimes I can't tell the good guys from the bad."

"Occupational hazard," Fasi says, laughing. "Sometimes the difference is almost imperceptible. We've no illusions. But there are gray areas in almost every profession, wouldn't you agree?"

"Frankly, I wouldn't."

"Then you're naïve, my young friend," Fasi says, not unkindly. "Totally understandable. But be assured that while we swim in a sea of sharks, always with potential dangers, we regard ourselves as the good guys, without question. Are there are moments of ambiguity? Of course, as when a bribe or some other persuasion may be necessary. But you find that in corporate or government life, as well, don't you?"

"At Princeton, we assumed that everybody in American business and government is beyond suspicion."

Fasi laughs out loud.

"No halos in real life, I'm afraid," Maurice puts in. "You'll learn that soon enough."

The idea had crossed my mind when we heard the Germans were using poison gas in the trenches.

"Yeah, I'm getting the picture."

"They didn't tell you at Princeton that your own government handed out smallpox blankets to Plains

Indians in an attempt to wipe out whole tribes?" Maurice asks.

"I didn't believe it when I read it."

"Historical fact. When you read about three hundred years of slavery, do you believe that?"

"A hard truth, I'll admit. But hardly unique to the US. Growing up we never even thought about it. Still don't."

"The lesson here is that sometimes we see only what we want to see," Fasi says. "We rewrite history and create fairy tales so we won't have to face facts."

"I confess my own grandfather was what you would call a robber baron," I say, surprised at my sudden willingness to bare all. "And that's a fact."

"Felix Kilgalen," Fasi pipes right up. "I had the pleasure of doing business with himself."

"What? When was that? Why?"

"Not to worry," Fasi reassures me. "Strictly legitimate. One of the original silent partners back in the late 1880s, in the early days of the syndicate. I was a young man then, new to the business myself."

"Why didn't you tell me you knew him?"

"Does it matter? I know a lot about a lot of people."

"It would've been nice to know you did business with my relative."

"Did you know your great-great-grandfather was Vice President of the United States?"

"You've done your homework. Frankly, that makes me a little uncomfortable."

Fasi flashes a hugely broad grin that looks almost menacing. I can see one shiny gold tooth and another tooth with a sparkling diamond stud in it.

"Just a routine precaution," he says. "We take our working relationships very seriously."

"I don't know whether to be flattered or worried."

"I assure you," Maurice adds, "the only ones who have anything to fear are those who try to steal from us."

"Then I suppose it's a good thing that I'm not in this for the money."

The moment I say it, I realize I'm kidding myself.

"No matter. You'll be a very wealthy man in a very short amount of time, regardless," Fasi says.

Turning to Goesse, I ask: "Maurice, you say you've met El Gato?"

"Yes. I'm one of the few Westerners who has ever set eyes on him. One of the most colorful characters you'll ever meet. I met him just before the War. Very tall. For someone who leads a deliberately secretive life, it's as if he wants to be seen. Red turban, like a bullseye in a sea of white. Dresses like a sheik, with flowing white jalabiyas trimmed in gold and silver damask. He carries a silver jambiya dagger in a hand-tooled gold and leather belt. It's theatrical, really. Two Turkish bodyguards, twins, ways at his side. They carry pearl-inlaid British Enfield rifles."

"Can't get much more colorful than that," I say. "But how does he guarantee trust from his bodyguards, given the treacherous world you describe?"

"I'm told he holds their families in house arrest in Ankara, thirteen souls in all. They want for nothing. But should a breach of trust or good faith occur, any betrayal whatsoever, they will all be put to death. And they know it."

"Sorry I asked. Obviously a man capable of terrible things. But how is he, I mean personally? What is he like face to face, as a person?"

"Face to face doesn't exactly apply. Legend has it that he's cordial, aristocratic, well educated. They say fluent in six languages, a gentleman and memorable persona by any measure," Maurice says. "But nobody in the consortium really knows, because he never speaks."

"Never speaks?"

"All communication is in written form. Letters, dispatches, fiats, coded messages. That sort of thing."

"How strange...He must have a great deal to hide."

"Just secretive, I reckon."

"How did you come to meet him, Maurice?"

"By accident. I was on my first visit to the mines, before the War. I was taking inventory in the central field office, standing at the at the mouth of the entrance. He came up behind me, never made a sound. There was this resplendent figure, flanked by his bodyguards. I was stunned. I'd been told never to expect to lay eyes on him. At that time, he wore a mask in the Moorish style, so I could see only the eyes."

"Were you living in Africa at the time?" I ask.

"Yes. I'd served in a Belgian regiment, and I'd been living in Congo for several years. I deserted one day and began passing myself off as a Belgian aristocrat in Brazzaville. So I had no trouble gaining access to the homes of wealthy colonials, who were only too happy to have a little royalty to show off. They never suspected it was I who stole their diamonds. But that's how I first got into the diamond business."

"You mean you were a *real* jewel thief?" I say, slightly taken aback. "What was that like?"

"Surprisingly agreeable. Eventually I was good enough, and made enough, to become a speculator myself."

"You see," adds Fasi, "this is how careers are made. Always a thin line between the legitimate and the illegitimate."

"Mind you, I made a serious miscalculation with my first partner," Maurice continues. "He was a Boer by the name of Van Hecht. He and I fell in love with the same girl. Gerti was her name. She worked in a colonial shop that traded in silks and diamonds. One night, Van Hecht showed up intoxicated and caught us in bed together. He flew into a rage and drew a pistol. Fortunately for me--but not so much for Van Hecht--I was the sniper in my old regiment. Of course, this incident necessitated a quick exit from Congo. I eventually came to the attention of the syndicate, and to Fasi."

He makes a small nod of the head to Fasi.

"What do we do now?" I ask him.

"We go to Fucauma."

I look at Maurice.

"Now it looks like we're both refugees."

He grins.

"It would appear so."

"Ah, Fucauma!" the merchant interjects. "Music to my ears! Delights my heart every time I hear that magic word. A successful mission to Fucauma is always worth a blessing, a celebration. For that, I know just the thing!"

He snaps his gold-encrusted fingers. The eunuch, ever attentive and never far away, appears with a bottle of whiskey on a silver tray.

"Could that be whiskey?" I ask, genuinely surprised.

"Whiskey? Whiskey's far too coarse a word to describe such a nectar of the gods," Fasi says. "This is not whiskey, child. This is Macallan single malt, fifty years in the barrel, the choice of kings and robber barons and Mustapha Fasil! Worth its weight in gold."

"And diamonds?"

"And diamonds," Fasi echoes with a little laugh.

"Pardon me, Fasi," I say, "but am I mistaken in assuming that Mohammedans do not drink alcohol?"

"Allah will always forgive a weakness," he tells me. "Many devout Muslims enjoy a glass of wine, or even whiskey, in the privacy of their own homes."

The golden-brown liquid is poured gently into crystal glasses, the smokey aroma rising.

"To long life and good fortune!" the merchant declares. "Lots of fortune!"

We begin with appreciative sips, taking our time. When the glasses are empty, the merchant refills each in turn. Then, following his lead, we knock back the second glass in one swallow, marveling at the heat and punch, then repeat the process three times.

"You understand your adventure isn't without considerable danger," Fasi cautions me, becoming suddenly serious. "Diamonds themselves are dangerous. Sometimes they exact the ultimate price."

"How do you mean?"

"Africa's unforgiving," he says. "Many a young man has come to seek his fortune only to disappear."

"Disappear? Why would they disappear?"

"Greed," Fasi says. "Greed and betrayal. Betrayal and greed. It's the same old story and it always ends badly. But I'm confident your story will have a happy ending, Max!"

He refills our glasses and we down another shot.

When we take our leave moments later, I almost walk into the wall.

"What an amateur!" Fasi says to Maurice. "You'll need to keep an eye on him."

6

The road to Marrakesh is no more than a camel track winding through vast stretches of rock, scrub, and sand. We ride for days on horseback, wrapped in hooded burnooses against scorching sun by day, frigid cold by night. Maurice, long familiar with the desert, is at peace in this strange, lonely stillness. But I'm lost in a hostile, alien wilderness, bemoaning the self-inflicted misery, too absorbed in my own discontent and discomfort to notice the beauty and natural wonders all around.

It brings back all the pain I had to endure with Andre Chirac.

We collect pallets of sundried camel dung off the desert floor to make fires and keep an eye out for any creature that might present an opportunity to supplement our daily rations of couscous, pistachios, dried fruit and goat cheese.

On the third night we make camp in an oasis with fresh water and grass for the horses. I'm wrapped in my burnoose, reclining against my Arabian saddle, counting stars in the diamond-studded desert sky, when I hear Maurice say: "Do not move. Do not move a muscle."

I stop breathing, never take my eyes off the stars.

The next thing, the night splits into a thunderous explosion, followed by a light spritz of sand and grit on my lap and on my face.

"It's okay now."

I let out my breath and lower my gaze. Looking down, I see the headless body of a snake between my legs. I can smell the cordite.

"It's an asp, a big one. He was starting to curl up in your crotch to keep warm," Maurice says, cradling in his hands a huge Parabellum handgun. "That's why it was so important you didn't move. If I'd missed I'd have shot off your balls or he'd have bitten you in the balls. Either way, not good."

"Great shot. You blew his head off."

The shock makes my voice shaky and unrecognizable.

Maurice walks over, reaches down, and lifts the body of the snake up into the firelight.

"That's because we're going to have him for dinner," he says. "Better than chicken. Welcome to desert life."

When we finally arrive in Marrakesh at the end of the fourth day, the entire village is coming awake with an inner glow of flickering candlelight, transforming humble mud brick buildings into fairy castles. Blue-robed Berbers just off the desert have set up camps in the spacious souk, each tribe with its own fire sending sparks spiraling up into the heavens. Some of the men dance to the rhythm of drums and tambourines. Pigeons and goat hearts roast in the open flames, filling the air with tantalizing aromas.

Men wave as we pass by.

"Salamo alaykom!" Maurice calls out, waving back.

Peace be upon you.

"'Ana 'uhibu 'khuyulak!" someone shouts.

I like your horses.

"Horses are a rare sight here. They always attract a little too much attention because they're prized as status symbols of wealth and power. We'll have to be on the alert against thieves," Maurice warns.

Moments later at the gate of a walled compound we're greeted by a white-robed Arab with a bolt-action Mauser slung over his shoulder.

"Ahlau bik!" the Arab says, crossing his hands on his chest and bowing slightly as a sign of respect.

Welcome.

"Kayf halukum?" Maurice answers.

How are you?

The guard opens the gate. We ride through, and the gate closes behind us.

"You're about to meet a true prince among men," Maurice says quietly. "Sheik Abdul Asim Arsalan Assad, the lion of the desert."

Before us appears an impressive figure robed entirely in black. Maurice and the sheik exchange a few words in Arabic. We dismount and grooms immediately lead the horses away. When the Sheik turns to me, I see the eyes in his sun-tanned face are a stunning bright blue.

"I understand you're a young man with a thirst for adventure, Mr. Kilgalen," he says in perfect Oxford English. I doubt that he can be more than a few years older than I am.

"Well sir, I suppose I am," I say, "but I'm new to all this and I've got a lot to learn."

"It's not like the eating clubs at Princeton or the debutante balls and teas, is it?"

"No, sir."

"You're far from home," the Sheik says, "but you're in good hands with Maurice. You can learn from him. I trained him myself. Now please come," he says, turning. "You must have an appetite after your long journey."

As we walk, Maurice cautions me in a whisper: "Remember, no forks or knives. And never touch the food with your left hand."

Inside the citadel with walls five feet thick we sit on silk cushions in a carpeted hall with a false tent ceiling and attendants in turbans hovering nearby. After a brief round of hot tea, we dig into an enormously satisfying meal of roast lamb, fresh figs, couscous, dried fruit, nuts, yogurt, pomegranate juice, hummus, honey, and pita bread, accompanied by several bottles of fine French wine, of which the sheik does not partake personally. But he keeps a full glass at hand to offer toasts.

"Hafiz Ak Allah," he says, raising his glass to us, taking a token taste.

May God protect you.

We reply in kind.

"Hafiz Ak Allah."

"The base at the massif is secure," the sheik tells Maurice as the meal commences. "I saw to that myself. We had an incident with Tuareg bandits who tried to ambush us. But we lost not a single man. It did not go so well for the Tuaregs."

During the conversation I discover that the sheik is not Berber but Arab Bedouin, and that he serves as the syndicate's enforcer throughout the region. After a second glass of the excellent wine, my curiosity emboldens me.

"Sir, if I may ask you a personal question?"

Maurice shoots me a look.

"What's your question?" the sheik asks.

"One can't help but notice the color of your eyes. Striking, really. Blue? Such a bright blue. To what do you attribute this most unusual trait?"

The sheik pauses. For an awful moment I'm afraid I may have gone too far.

But then he smiles broadly.

"I'm happy to answer your question. My mother is a celebrated Englishwoman who came to be known here as Edwina, Queen of the Desert. Her real name is Lady Edwina Langdon, Duchess of Cornwall. She first came to the Levant as a young woman to assist her father, my grandfather, the Duke, who was an amateur archaeologist collecting rare historical relics for the British Museum.

"Edwina was just seventeen when she met my father, Sheik Fasil Al-Hab bin Sadr, at a British embassy ball in Medina. He was tall, very handsome, spoke excellent English. They fell in love. But her father forbade it. So they ran off and she became his first wife and remains his favorite to this day, though they are often apart. When I was old enough to attend a boarding school back in England, she was snubbed by her family. So after two years we returned to Arabia, where she was formally welcomed into the Bedouin tribe. So now you know why my eyes are blue."

"Edwina, such a beautiful name. I've read about your mother, haven't I?" I say. "I remember seeing a photograph of her with T. E. Lawrence, both of them on camels."

"Lawrence and my mother fought together against the Turks," the sheik says. "She provided information to British intelligence and Lawrence and my father blew up bridges and trains. My father and I led calvary charges against Turkish positions. He was shot off his horse right next to me but survived to ride again."

The sheik pours more wine into our glasses.

"And didn't your mother herself once narrowly escaped capture?"

"That's true. A Turkish patrol quite accidently stumbled upon her camp and demanded that all the women assemble. Then they demanded that the woman by the name of Edwina step forward and identify herself. At that, every woman stepped forward. The Turks became agitated, demanding that the women remove their burkas and reveal their faces. When no one complied, a Turkish officer stepped forward and raised his hand to strike one of the women. My mother shot him, then the other five soldiers in quick succession. Apparently, they weren't expecting a woman who knew how to handle a gun."

There's a moment of reflection as the image sinks in.

"Remarkable woman, your mother, truly an historic figure," I say, admiringly.

"Truth be told, she's an historic figure but also something of a mystery, even to her own family. Even to this day."

"How so?"

"She was always unpredictable and eccentric, with an insatiable need for extreme adventure, even danger," the sheik explains. "One day years ago she simply left my father and disappeared without explanation into the desert. Rumors began to spread of a Queen of the Desert who led a small private army that chased down and assassinated any warlord who threatened peace and stability in the region. To some tribes she was hailed as a godlike heroine, to others as a terrifying angel of death. The family in England disavowed her. My father turned his back on her. He forbade the mention of her name in his presence."

I listen in amazement.

"If I may ask, how do you feel about all that?"

The sheik thinks for a moment.

"As a son, I am concerned for her safety," he says. "But she's shown she's more than capable of taking care of herself. What concerns me more is the elaborate secrecy that surrounds her life. Now she's disappeared again. There's a rumor she's somewhere in Mali, probably Timbuktu."

"What would she be doing there?"

"I'm told she's now in the diamond trade. For all I know, she may even be part of the consortium. What do you think, Maurice?"

Maurice appears nonplussed.

"I'm always the last to know these things," he says. "Your guess is as good as mine."

"Mystery woman," the sheik mutters. He nods in acceptance and pours the last of the third bottle of wine into our glasses.

"My complements to you, once again, Abdul Asim, on your excellent table," Maurice says. "That was a memorable feast."

"Ah, but's it's not over yet," the sheik says, producing a plate of chocolates. "As it happens, I have access to the finest chocolate in the world, originally produced by a nouveau riche chocolatier, a man known to me only by his nickname, Le Gros. He built a chocolate empire which gave him the means to also build a marble mansion in Parc Monceau in

Paris. My mother once kept a home there, as well. I met him, oddly, not in Paris, but in Africa."

"What was a chocolatier doing in Africa?" Maurice asks.

"A very strange tale that begins with a prima ballerina from the Bolshoi, Ilena Broskova, who married the man for his money."

"Nothing strange about that," I venture.

"The chocolatier was so smitten by his ballerina that he gave her carte blanche to create an oasis of earthly delights here in Africa, the kind of exotic Belle Epoch private retreat that might attract European aristocracy, royalty, and celebrity guests from all over the world. She planned to name her dream paradise Le Serpent D'Or, the Golden Snake. Le Gros wound up buying two thousand hectares sight unseen from a local Berber tribe. Of course, the tribe never owned the land in the first place. Nobody did. So what he really bought was protection against plunder."

The sheik pauses to rinse his hands in a silver bowl filled with rose-scented lemon water, passing the bowl on to his guests. We dry our hands with linen towels offered by turbaned servants.

"Alas, the plan was never to be," the sheik continues. "Unfortunately, the chocolatier had a glutton's passion for haute cuisine. He became a minor celebrity due to his culinary eccentricities and morbid obesity. People would turn out on the streets of Paris to cheer him on to his next gluttonous conquest, shouting, 'Vive Le Gros! Vive Le Gros!'

"Well, one night Le Gros bit off more than even he could chew. In the midst of a bet that he could devour more than a thousand oysters in twenty minutes, he inhaled one. Witnesses say it wasn't until his five-chinned face turned a deathly blue that anyone realized something had gone wrong. In one massive motion, he suddenly pitched forward, sending oysters, crystal, silverware, and bottles of the best champagne cascading to the parquetted floor. Horrified onlookers scrambling everywhere trying to save their white ties and patent leather shoes."

"What happened to the ballerina?" I ask.

"She took up with a wealthy banker living next door in Parc Monceau, with whom she'd already been having an affair."

"No surprises there, either" Maurice says.

"To satisfy her personal needs, she kept a single employee to continuously make chocolates for her exclusive consumption. After she died, I managed to arrange for that extremely limited supply to come to me and to me alone."

7

In the morning, the sheik bids us farewell. Our handsome Arabian horses are fully rested and prepared. We set off with an armed escort that takes us through the streets of Marrakesh to the southern gate. About a mile beyond, the escort turns back, leaving us to continue our journey alone. Somewhere along the road that leads over the Atlas Mountains to the remote base the syndicate calls the Citadel, a lone rider on camelback suddenly emerges out of a dry wadi, blocking our way.

Maurice and the rider exchange a few words in Arabic.

"He's a Berber. He wants to talk to us about our horses," Maurice says. Then under his breath he adds: "He intends to rob us. He's not alone."

I couldn't have known it at the time, but I was about to learn my first lesson in desert survival.

"What do we do?" I ask.

"Be prepared for gunplay. But let me try something first."

Then he speaks again to the man.

"I've invited him to come over to have a closer look at the horses. When he dismounts, so do we. But move slowly. Look relaxed."

The camel bellows and sinks to its forelegs. As the Berber eases himself out of the saddle, so do we.

The Berber approaches, peers into the mouths of the horses, then produces a pistol and addresses Maurice menacingly. In a flash, Maurice disarms the man and spins him into a death lock. I grab the loose gun and jam it into the belt of my kaftan robe. With his other hand, Maurice presses the barrel of his Parabellum hard against the would-be robber's head. The bandit sinks to his knees as two more armed riders on camels appear from the dry wadi, rifles at the ready.

Maurice tightens his choke hold and says something urgently to the bandit, then loosens his grip long enough for the man to bark out an order.

"Alwugut wa'linsak niranik!"

Stand down. Hold your fire!

The men lower their rifles.

Maurice continues his one-way conversation with the would-be thief, who, still fast in a chokehold and unable to speak, can only nod. After several minutes, Maurice releases his grip and lowers his pistol. The Berber, still on his knees, calls out again to his men.

"Lagad tsaeahadt bialshavat!"

I have pledged a vow of honor!

The riders slowly slide their rifles back into their saddle scabbards. The Berber bends to place his hands upon Maurice's boots, then rises to his feet, his hands crossed on his chest, and salaams three times before re-mounting his camel and returning to his men.

"Now there'll be gunfire," Maurice alerts me. "Don't shoot. It's merely a salute."

As he speaks, the riders all withdraw their rifles and fire into the air three times.

Then they turn and ride back towards Marrakesh.

"What was that all about?" I ask nervously as we get back on our horses. "Why did we let him go? He could've killed us both."

"Of course. But you never know when you might need an ally," Maurice replies. "The Berbers may be bandits, but they're also men of honor. To make such a pledge as the Berber just made to me, and then violate that pledge would bring shame and disgrace upon him, his family and tribe. Honor's everything. That's the first thing you learn about this part of Africa. Everything's based on honor."

"That's good to know."

"It could save your life."

"Do you think more of these fellows will show up?"

"Not where we're going. The sheik took care of the Tuareg bandits who typically haunt the mountains."

Ahead looms our next destination, the mighty, snow-capped Atlas range.

That night we camp in a high pass. The air's sweet, the water snowmelt-pure, and the abundantly wild grasses are a lush emerald green. Maurice builds a fire and sets the horses out to graze while I brave a plunge into an ice-fed rushing stream, splashing around just long enough to wash away dust and grime from three days of sweaty travel.

Before dawn, with horses well fed and rested and waterbags full to bursting, we press on to take advantage of cool morning temperatures.

"We should arrive at the Citadel before sundown," Maurice announces as we pull out.

"Who's this fellow we're supposed to meet?" I ask. The horses are picking their way with care along a treacherously narrow piste as we climb slowly to the top of the final rise, about a mile ahead.

"His official title is The Right Honorable Sir Basil Wesley-Rhodes, Marquis of Salisbury, Protector of the Treasury and Guardian of the Great Seal," Maurice answers. "We just call him The Banker. He's the master of the Citadel, apparently the only person in the world El Gato trusts to administer the Syndicate's massive wealth."

"He's European?"

"Yes. A bit theatrical. They all are. But not like El Gato! Once you meet him, you'll never forget him. He's got an amazing story to tell. He may choose to share it with you. When we first met, he told me. It's quite a tale."

"What exactly does he do?"

"He oversees most of the Western World's diamond traffic. On any given day, he presides over several billion dollars' worth of product."

"You're talking about just diamonds?"

"Diamonds and cash in multiple denominations across international clientele. Incoming and outgoing, up and down this main trade artery connecting Africa and Europe. Eighty-five percent of the world's diamonds pass through the Citadel."

"How much of that trade is legitimate?"

"I don't know, and I don't ask. But I do know that it involves governments, businesses, institutions, private investors, shady dealers, even the black market, you name it."

"What about Orthodox Jews? I thought they control the diamond trade in Europe and the US?"

"Only by the grace of El Gato and the Syndicate are they even permitted in the game. But at a price. They have to pay to play."

"Sounds like a criminal organization to me."

"It depends on how you define criminal. It's just a business, like any other," Maurice says evenly.

"Hardly like any other."

"As Fasi said, pull back the lid on any corporation or government and take a good look inside. It's not necessarily a pretty sight."

"I don't understand how it works. Surely there must be thousands of people up and down the supply and distribution chains. This can't be the work of just one or two men."

"No doubt. But who they are and where they are and how they operate is known only to the Sheik, El Gato, and The Banker."

"And what about competition?" I persist. "Diamonds are a global business. Surely the Syndicate can't operate in a total vacuum outside the global network."

"Of course not. There are four other major players, but they all answer to the Syndicate," Maurice replies. "De Beers in Luxembourg and South Africa. British and Australian Rio Tinto. Alrosa in Russia. And of course Bharat Diamond Bourse in India, which serves much of the Middle East, South Asia, and the Orient. Each of these diamond monoliths is subservient to the Syndicate. They're allowed to function only under strict protocols dictated by El Gato himself."

"You'd need an army of enforcers to control such large enterprises," I protest. "How is it even possible?"

"Only a handful of people have the answers. For myself, I've learned to understand that what appears to be impossible can often turn out to be quite possible. Knowing that, I've come to accept things as they are."

"Aren't you curious? Don't you even want to know?"

"Not particularly. What good would it do?"

We ride on in silence.

Maurice has become a conundrum.

Who is he, really?

As we crest the top of the mountain, we catch the first flash of day. I glance over my shoulder, blinded by an explosion of light slicing across the edge of the world, welcome warmth against a long night of cold mountain air.

I turn my horse and stop to watch the sun slowly illuminate snow-capped peaks all around.

"This is truly a wonder," I say, awed by the sight.

Maurice stops his horse.

"I've seen it a few times," he says. "If you ask me, nothing can compare to diamonds."

Then we turn and pick our way down the far side of the massif. The horses navigate with delicate caution along steep mountain drops and dizzying precipices. They falter several times, nearly losing their footing entirely in two shallow but fast-moving rivers.

A high valley slops gently down through foothills toward a grassy plain far below. Finally, at the end of the day, with shadows lengthening, we pause on a broad ledge with unobstructed views up and down the valley.

"Quite a view," I say. "You can see forever."

"That's why our central transfer station is here."

"I don't see it."

"Of course not. Come this way." Maurice turns his horse and stops in front of a towering wall of granite.

"This is the only land route from Timbuktu to European markets. Anyone who wants to be in the game has to pass through these mountains."

I glance up and see an armed guard waving from a rocky outcrop far above. I spot a second guard. Then a third.

There's a grumbling, grinding sound as a thick slab of rock the size of a barn door begins to swing outward, revealing a hidden entrance. Maurice leads his horse through the opening, and I follow. Inside, a shaft of natural light from somewhere high above illuminates a large circular chamber. Two men appear and take our horses down a spacious side corridor lit with electric lights. I trail Maurice towards an enormous set of metal doors on the far side of the chamber. Two armed guards open them, and we step into a well-lit, carpeted space the size of a ballroom. European antique furniture adorns an impressive library of thousands of books. The far end of the room features a massive fireplace hewn from living rock. Fresh, pine-scented mountain air from outside circulates like a cool breeze throughout. I detect the muted hum of a generator emanating from somewhere deep inside the mountain.

"This was once a natural cave system," Maurice tells me. "It's one of the most secure locations in the world."

A door opens and a large Caucasian man enters the room wearing a gilded black silk kaftan decorated with gold-threaded French fleurs-de-lis. His head is crowned with a diamond-encrusted white turban.

Maurice makes the formal introduction.

"You may call me Sir Basil," the big man says, extending his hand. "It's a pleasure to see a new face."

"Thank you, sir," I reply. "I learn something new every day."

"Indeed! Truer words never spoken. So much to learn. But I've been here as long as you've been alive, and I've still not unlocked all the secrets."

"Secrets, sir?"

"Oh yes, my boy! It's all about secrets. Everything's a secret. Maurice can tell you about that."

I glance at Maurice. He shrugs dismissively, as if he's heard it all.

"Please, sit down," As we take our seats, Sir Basil says:

"American?"

"Yes, sir."

"Lafayette Escadrille?"

"Yes. Americans in the French Air Service. But the War was over before I could fly any missions."

"Shame. But I'm sure the organization can make use of your flying skills. I would certainly expect so, particularly since Emilio Carrado Sanchez, the man known to you as El Gato, is an aviation fanatic and is reportedly building a private fleet of flying machines in Spain."

"If true, that's exciting news."

I glance at Maurice. He gives me the nod.

"Speaking of El Gato, sir, we're trying to track down the missing treasure stolen by Baron Sehrgitz. Since El Gato was said to be the sole point of contact for the Baron, he may be the key to recovering the hidden stash, if there is one."

"Very hard fellow to pin down, El Gato," Sir Basil says. "He was here not a fortnight ago on one of his regular visits. Of course, I didn't get to see him personally. As is his custom, he remained silent. We communicated through messages passed back and forth. As I say, we operate in a culture of secrecy. All transactions with the Baron were secret, also. As for myself, if I knew the answer to your question, I wouldn't tell you, because it could cost me my life. All I can tell you is that El Gato continued to authorize distribution to the Baron until the end of the War. Beyond that, I can tell you nothing."

"Can you tell us the total amount of disbursements to the Baron?"

"It was something in the order of fifty million dollars, give or take."

"More give or more take?"

Maurice gives me a side look.

"I can get you the precise figure."

"That would be helpful."

Later, in a candle-lit room paneled entirely in mirrors, with multiple images of ourselves diminishing with magical effect into infinity, we sit down to a hearty meal of duck, lamb, couscous, pomegranates, pistachios, French cheeses, and of course the fine French wines to which I'm becoming accustomed.

In the course of the conversation, Maurice reminisces with Sir Basil about his early life as a novice jewel thief.

The Banker smiles and nods appreciatively. He fills his glass and takes another sip.

"And you, my boy," the Banker says, turning to me, "Are you a jewel thief, too?"

"I suppose I am," I reply. "I never thought I'd hear myself say that."

"Don't feel too badly," he says. "I see a bright future for you. You'll someday be very wealthy. And then you can indulge yourself the luxury of becoming a philanthropist and benefactor. There is no such thing as good and bad. But that of course is entirely up to you."

I think about that for a moment.

"Thank you, Sir Basil. But if I had to judge my current situation, I'd say I'm somewhere between a would-be Wall Streeter and would-be soldier of fortune. Untested in either. The robes hide the real me. You could say I'm a work in progress. So I've no idea who I really am."

Sir Basil nods appreciatively.

"It's a bit of a drama, isn't it?" he says. "As the Bard so wisely put it, we're all but actors upon a stage, each of us with secrets we share with no one."

An attendant steps up and refills our glasses.

"However, I'm prepared to share a few secrets of my own with you this very night, if you're inclined to hear them," the banker says, clearly enjoying the company.

We both signal enthusiastic consent.

"Very well, then! To begin, let me say that the man you see before you now is a far cry from the boy I once was," the Banker begins. "My father, the sixth Marquis, drank and gambled away his birthright, leaving my mother penniless to raise her children and beg employment from her former social friends. I fled to America, without funds, but fortune smiled, and eventually I ended up a Maître d' in St Louis, an English accent being highly regarded in the hinterlands.

"It was there that I made the acquaintance of an English peer, Sir Edward Ashley Haddington-Rhodes, who had known my father and was in America on a lark to see the Wild West and shoot bison. He asked if I'd like to join him. Of course, I jumped at the chance.

"The next morning in the club car of the Sportsman's Special Pacific Railroad train I was enjoying a fantasy breakfast come true: caviar, smoked trout, Earl Grey tea, scones, and poached eggs. That's how I began my new life as the youngest bison hunter in the history of the West. At the time it seemed like a great adventure. But I later came to see the whole episode as a terrible, shameful thing. Day after day the train would roll slowly through the middle of endless herds of thousands of buffalo, with armed passengers at every open window on both sides unleashing fusillade after fusillade of heavy fire into the poor beasts. They fell like flies, left to rot on the open plains. How does one forgive such unsportsmanlike behavior among the grown men and women who engaged with such delight in this infamous mass slaughter? It's perhaps a revealing window into the dark nature of man. Loathsome as it was, it was to me the greatest adventure I could ever have imagined."

He empties his wine glass.

"When we eventually reached our destination of Denver, Colorado," he continues, "my distinguished benefactor, Sir Edward, was greeted on the station platform by none other than the celebrated William Frederick Cody, 'Buffalo Bill', who'd been engaged by Sir Edward for a private trophy hunt for elk in the high Rockies. To my surprise and delight, I was included in the hunt.

"I got to know Buffalo Bill as well as one can know anyone in so short a time. He confided many stories around the campfire. He talked about how he became a rider for the Pony Express at just age fifteen, and about his experiences in the Union Army in the Civil War, and how he served as a scout in the Indian Wars, winning the Medal of Honor. He had plans, he said, to soon start a road show he intended to call *Buffalo Bill's Wild West,* about his legendary exploits all over the American West.

"He started calling me 'Buster' because he was going to teach me how to bust broncos, and 'Sport' because he knew I was a good shot. But the most interesting thing he confided to me, one night after Sir Edward had retired to his tent, was the secret cache of diamonds he had liberated from a Confederate mail train during the Civil War."

"Diamonds?"

"Yes. An enormous sum in an always negotiable quantity, part of a last-gasp effort to finance the South in its desperate final days. But the mail train was intercepted by Mr. Cody and his scouts, who never bothered to report the find to the North. Without the diamonds, the South, whose fiat currency was failing, was forced to capitulate. Thereby many lives were spared. But the proud South was broken. Buffalo Bill told me he hid the diamonds in a cave in Arkansas and had plans to someday to put them to good use. So, Max, it turns out Buffalo Bill was a jewel thief, too. You're in good company."

There's a pause as I grapple with that.

Can it be true?

"Sir, do you mean to say this is factual?" I respond with no attempt to disguise my skepticism. "Frankly, I find it hard to believe. I've never heard that story before."

"That's because it's not in any history books."

"What happened to the diamonds?"

"Well, it turned out that be never did retrieve them."

"Why not? How do you know he didn't?"

"I'm not sure why he didn't. But we stayed in touch over the years. In time, I became like a son and he like the father I never knew. Before he died, I was handed a sealed envelope, with detailed instructions on how to find them."

"He gave the diamonds to you?"

"He wanted to assure they were in good hands before his death. So I set out on a journey to find the diamonds with Buffalo Bill's instructions in hand. They were precisely where the instructions said they would be."

"What did you do with them?"

"That must remain my secret. But I can tell you that when it comes to El Gato and diamonds, there are no secrets, and nothing escapes his attention."

"El Gato knew."

"He found me, and to put it simply, he made me an offer I couldn't refuse."

"Surely with the amount of money you're talking about, you would be beholden to no one and able to refuse anything..."

"So you might imagine. But the reality is very different. In the end the diamonds bought me a seat at the table within the Syndicate. Sadly, my mother had since died. But with just a few of the many thousands of gems now in my possession, I was able to restore the family titles, buy back the family estates, and provide for my brother and sister. Over the years, my regret for the misfortunes that befell them has always been a source of endless grief."

His eyes reflect genuine sorrow.

"What did you do with the rest?"

"They're in a very safe place, I can assure you. Enough diamonds to make me one of the richest men in the world."

"Then why are you here in a cave in Africa instead of a palazzo in Italy or a villa on the French Rivera?"

The Banker chuckles. He takes another sip.

"Excellent question!" he says. "It's complicated, more complicated than you can imagine. Once you enter into a business relationship with El Gato you stay in that relationship. All I can say is that I've been entrusted with a great responsibility, hand-picked by El Gato himself, and I'm performing a service. It's an honor. And I intend to fulfill my obligations."

"If you had to guess, where do you think we might find El Gato?" Maurice asks.

"He was on his way to Timbuktu when I last saw him. Not that I actually saw him," the Banker says. "Beyond that, the only one who knows is El Gato himself. They don't call him the ghost for nothing."

8

When Helmut Knauss first notices something wrong, it's almost too late. He feels a slight falter in the gait of the mule he's riding, enough to get his attention and cause him to look back. At the end of a twenty-foot rope attached to his saddle, he sees that his Tuareg slave has stumbled and fallen. She's being dragged through the Saharan scrabble, her black jalaba, burnoose and hajib filthy from desert dirt. But when the mule stops, she struggles onto her feet.

The German dismounts and begins to beat her with a riding crop, bellowing in German. The woman holds her ground, slashing at his face with her hands, which only enrages him more.

By the time we arrive on the scene, he's punching her with his fists, but she's still fighting, deflecting his blows, refusing to fall.

"What the hell's going on?" I ask Maurice.

"Don't interfere. I know this guy. He's a deserter, like me. He's crazy and dangerous. We served together for a short time as mercenaries. The woman's his slave. The story goes he found her wandering the desert. She'd been sold to the king of some tribe. The king abused her. So she killed him and fled the tribe. The German took her in as a slave, but she's also his wife. He has every right to abuse her. If we interfere, he'll try to kill us. We don't want trouble. Just ride on by."

That's when the German, dressed in a fraying German Army uniform stained with dust and sweat, pauses from beating the woman. His sun-browned, unshaven face is furious.

"What the fuck are you looking at?" he roars defiantly in broken English, his eyes wild with rage. "Mind your own fucking business!"

At that, he pulls out a Luger pistol and turns back toward to the woman.

"Stay calm," Maurice says. "Let's go..."

The German wheels toward us and shoots. Maurice returns fire. The German takes a step back, looks at his abdomen, then raises his pistol to take aim again.

"Finish him."

I fire, hitting the German in the chest. He sinks to his knees, then slowly pitches face down into the dirt.

"That's number two," Maurice says. "Pretty soon all the bad guys will fear you."

As we approach, the woman, in a defiant stance, pulls back her cowl, revealing a strikingly beautiful face. She's clearly not Tuareg. Middle Eastern, perhaps? Her dark eyes are fiercely proud, signaling courage and a burning intelligence. I couldn't have identified it at the time, but several years later I'd recognize the legendary queen Nefertiti in that face. Her celebrated likeness would soon emerge intact after almost three and a half thousand years from the tomb of Egyptian boy-Pharaoh Tutankhamun.

"You happy now?" Maurice says to me. "I can tell you she's not happy."

"We just saved her life."

"You don't understand. However sorry her lot, now she's got nothing. She's thinks we're going to kill her. If we don't, she'll probably kill herself. Besides, she's no better than a common whore, no good to anyone."

"How can you say that?"

"Because she's been used and abused. I know something about whores. Seen it all before."

"I'll bet you've never seen anyone like that."

I can't take my eyes off her face.

"She's got looks, I'll give you that," he says. "I wouldn't mind fucking her. Maybe I will."

The woman watches warily as I go through the German's pockets, producing a wad of Belgian and French francs and a bundle of almost worthless German deutschmarks. There's also a pocketknife, military ID, and a worn leather wallet with a photo of a singularly unattractive woman with the face of a bulldog. We appropriate the Luger, a Mauser rifle and ammunition, a small tin of Belgian chocolates, and a Bayard service pistol with two boxes of shells. Then we dig a shallow grave and roll the German in.

The woman watches intently.

I step toward her, captivated. The powerful attraction's more than beauty. Maurice dismisses her as a lowly primitive. But I sense natural nobility and admirable inner strength.

She doesn't flinch.

There's an exotic, earthy smell of sweat and spices. Cloves? Cinnamon?

Scent of a woman.

Now I can see that her eyes, full in the light of the sun, glint with traces of turquoise, cobalt blue, coal black, even lilac and purple.

Nefertiti.

I'm hopelessly smitten.

How could so rare a beauty end up trapped in degradation, danger, and hopelessness?

I feel a blazing desire to protect her.

She boldly holds my gaze as I reach out and gently wipe a drop of blood from the corner of her lips. She says something unknowable, her voice mesmerizing, rich as wild honey.

I can't understand what she's saying. Whatever it is, she reveals no fear.

"Snap out of it, man!!" Maurice barks, interrupting my reverie. "She might be a good fuck, but beyond that, don't get hooked. She wants to get you emotionally involved. She'll use her looks to try to get her way with you."

"Look at that face!" I say. "Maybe I wouldn't mind getting emotionally involved."

"Grow up, man! This isn't a game. This is Africa. You have everything. She has nothing. She just wants to use you. Why else would she flirt with you?"

"Maybe because I shot her worst nightmare? Maybe she's grateful! And maybe she likes what she sees."

"She wouldn't try that crap with me. These people are clever. She's smart enough to know just by looking at me that I can tell what she's up to. She knows I know."

I turn to him.

"Jesus, Maurice! You saw what he did to her? How can you blame her? How can we just walk away from this?"

"Listen to me!" he fairly shouts. "These people are by nature secretive and deceptive. You never know what they're really thinking."

"These people? You don't even know who or what she is! And maybe she's got a good reason to be secretive and deceptive."

"They're all the same to me," he says. "Bloody white man's burden! Give her a chance and she'll likely kill you and steal your money."

"I don't have any money. Does she look like she wants to kill me?"

"Feigned innocence can hide guilty intent. Naivete, if you're not careful, can wind up being your biggest enemy, and ultimately your downfall. That's all I have to say."

"So what would you have us do? Just leave her here?" I ask, becoming impatient. "We have to get her to safety, at least."

Nefertiti's eyes are moving back and forth between us, alert, attentive.

Calculating?

Can she understand what we're saying?

"OK." Maurice looks away. "She can come with us. Just don't get involved,"

I offer the woman my hand.

"Let's see what happens," I say to Maurice, assisting her onto the German's mule. "Maybe the first thing we do is get her a bath."

9

Hours later, we approach a campfire in the gathering dusk. We're met by armed men. Maurice speaks to them in Arabic. It turns out it's a camel caravan bedding down for the night. He gives them something from his saddle bag and continues the conversation. The men nod and smile appreciatively and welcome us to join them. We pitch a tent among the camels and start our own fire.

As we're collecting more dried camel dung, I ask, "What did you give that man?"

"A metal pin of a golden eagle, making him and his fellow tribesmen official members of the High Order of the Lafayette Escadrille."

"You gave him your pin?"

"I have fifty more. I requisitioned a whole box from the armory before we left France. They come in very handy, as you can see."

"These people are Dogons, nomads," Maurice explains. "They love trinkets and ceremony. We just had a little ceremony. It's our ticket, you might say, to join the safety of the armed caravan, which is always a good idea in the desert when the opportunity presents itself. Their camels are loaded with salt, spices, brassware, and probably leather goods they're hauling up to markets on the Med. It's a lucrative business. Some of this stuff, mostly salt, will wind up in Europe, where salt fetches a very high price."

"Salt in the desert?"

"Don't forget, this was all once the bottom of an ancient sea. But the salt doesn't come easy. You've got to break it up with sledgehammers and manhandle 200-pound slabs in 120 heat all day long with virtually no protection from the sun. Tuaregs do it and Dogons do it. Worst job in the world. But worth it because in some places it's worth its weight in gold."

Nefertiti remains silent, her eyes observing us cautiously from behind her hijab.

"If you're wondering about the tent, it's not for us, it's for her," Maurice adds. "We sleep outside. But since she's the only woman in the camp, she sleeps in a tent. It's customary."

"How can you be sure these people won't rob us and try to rape her?" I ask.

"No guarantees. But it comes down to honor. Once they accept a gift and welcome us, we become guests under their protection."

"Sounds like you've got a higher regard for these people."

"No. But at least I know what I'm dealing with. I don't think you have to worry."

"All the same, I think I'll sleep with my gun under my head."

We sit down for a light dinner of biltong, a South African beef jerky that Maurice carries in a canvas saddle bag. Nefertiti accepts a piece and gives me a sloe-eyed side look. Testosterone roars back in every cell of my body.

She turns and moves toward her tent to eat alone.

Maurice steps in front of her, blocking her path, and draws her into a rough embrace, clasping his hands on her buttocks.

She immediately recoils violently and struggles to escape.

"What are you doing?" I cry out.

Nefertiti brings her knee up, breaks free and bares her claws, defiant, prepared to stave off another advance.

"Just a bit of fun," Maurice jests, cupping his crotch and pretending to laugh it off. "She's a bit of a hellfire, that one. Just so you know, I intend to have some of that, whether we're going to sell her or not."

"Not if I can help it."

Nefertiti slips into her tent.

"You need to relax," Maurice says, taking his seat again by the fire. "You're losing perspective. There's a nice body under that jalaba."

"You think you can just rape her?"

"What of it?"

"Seriously? Rape her?"

"What are you going to do about it?"

"Maybe I'll kill you."

He glances at me with questioning eyes, tries to guess my level of conviction, then turns back to the fire and studies the flames.

After a few moments, he says: "Well, Max, I'd say that's a pretty short-sighted solution. You'd both be dead without me."

I stare into the flames with detachment and brood about my situation. Maurice has a point. There's no going back. I also find myself having to admit I've landed in a sorry predicament the likes of which I could never have anticipated.

Later, he asks: "You still thinking about your girlfriend in the tent?"

"Actually, I'm thinking about something else. You never told me you were part of a criminal organization."

He gives me a side look.

"Why does it matter?"

"Because now I'm part of this criminal thing, too. I never signed up for that."

"The worst thing that could happen would be that you'll be a millionaire many times over before you're thirty. And you'll thank me for that," he says. "Don't ask so many questions. I told you that you'd see your share of the diamonds and you will. You have to trust me. It's either that, or you're free to go anytime and try to make your way back home. But that's not where I'm going."

10

In the pale light of predawn, Nefertiti emerges from her tent. I give her a cup of tea, which she cradles in her hands as she watches us fold the tent, keeping a wary eye on Maurice. We stow the gear on the horses, break camp, kick dirt on the fire. I help her mount the mule and we head south toward Timbuktu, our horses trailing the mule in cool morning air.

We all remain silent.

"Does she have a name?" Maurice asks me after a while.

"If she does, she hasn't told me."

"Does she understand what you're saying?"

"I don't say much. I don't think so."

"Have you thought more about what we're going to do with her?"

"Yes, I was wondering about that."

"I was thinking we should sell her," he says.

"Are you serious?"

"You can see yourself how beautiful she is. She'd bring a good price."

"Sell her into slavery? Are you kidding?"

"You have a better idea? We could also rent her out as a whore."

"Jesus. Maurice!"

"What are we supposed to do?"

"We're supposed to do the right thing, and that doesn't include slavery. Or prostitution."

"Is that what they taught you at Princeton?"

"Something like that, yes."

"What if I were to tell you that maybe she wants to be a slave? Or a prostitute? What if slavery or selling her body is her only ticket to security? And because she murdered her husband maybe she wants to get lost, totally disappear."

"I don't understand how you can talk like that. She's a human being. She deserves our respect, yours and mine."

"Respect? Seriously? Maybe you don't understand how these people think. She knows she's in danger. She needs protection. It's a different world from the one you know."

"Nobody in their right mind wants to be a slave. Sell another human being? I couldn't live with that." I shake my head at the thought. "And technically, we don't own her. She isn't ours to sell."

He gives me a challenging look.

"Oh, so now we're concerned about property rights? Where do you get these ideas? You want to fuck her? Maybe she'll let you. Maybe she'll ask you for money. Then you'll know what I'm talking about. In the meantime, remember, she's got no place to go. If the king's tribe finds her, they'll probably kill her. She's got no one. No friends, no family, no hope. Except maybe someone who would step forward and buy her. At least then she could be fed and feel safe."

"Or wind up with another crazy animal like the German and be beaten to death."

We stop talking and ride on.

After a while I say, "All right. If slavery's the easiest solution, I'll buy her."

"What?"

"I'll buy her. But I'd never enslave her. She'd be free."

"You must be heat struck."

"It doesn't have to be forever. Maybe she'd like the idea. Why don't we ask her?"

I look back at the woman. She continues to watch us, rocking gently on the mule.

"Who are you going to buy her from?" Maurice asks. "She may be a former slave but she's free now."

"There must be a way," I say.

"The best way is to resist all temptation and stay the hell out of it. If she looked like the picture of that hag in the German's wallet would you be so enthusiastic? We're talking about a problem that's only going to get worse the longer it's allowed to linger. She's got to go."

We ride on.

After several minutes he says:

"There are things you don't know."

"What don't I know?"

He glances back at the lady on the mule.

"I'll let you in on a secret," he says. "I was going to save it as a surprise. We have an agent in Timbuktu."

"Why's that a surprise?"

"The agent is Edwina, Queen of the Desert."

"The sheik's mother?" I ask, incredulous. "He was right about his mother, then? She really is in Timbuktu?"

"Yes."

"Why the secrecy? Why does her own son have to be the last to know?"

"I can't answer that. All I know is, that's how this thing works. It's a house of secrets. Nobody knows anything. And it seems to work because if nobody knows anything, there's nothing to know."

"I thought she was living in a harem somewhere in Arabia."

"Or maybe England," he says. "Or maybe Paris. But right now she's in Timbuktu. You'll never meet another woman quite like her. As you'll see, she's old enough to be your mother. But she doesn't look a day over thirty-five."

"The sheik...?"

"He only thinks he knows. As I say, we operate in a world of secrets. He doesn't have to know."

"But it's his mother..."

"She keeps an eye on her son, and everyone else. Maybe she's in Timbuktu because nobody can keep an eye on her. But El Gato trusts her. They're close. I understand he often goes there. So she might be able to tell us what happened to the missing gems. If we're lucky, El Gato might be able to tell us himself. This is where my little personal secret comes in. You see, Edwina's more than just a business associate."

"You're screwing the sheik's mother?"

"The reason I'm letting you in on this because of her," he says, gesturing toward the woman. "Edwina can be unpredictable. She might not take kindly to another beautiful woman suddenly in the mix. We don't need more complications."

"I don't see complications in that. I see you with the sheik's mother and me with the lady on the mule."

"There's something else," he adds. "Edwina may also have her eye on you."

"On me? How does she even know about me?"

"You've been told about how this works – all things are known at the top."

I fall back until my horse is parallel with the mule. Nefertiti smiles, eyeing me steadily. Not flirtatious, just shy. Her mouth is full, inviting.

"Tu parle Francais?" I ask.

Do you speak French?

"Yes, I..." She stops herself. "I mean...oui..."

"You speak English?"

"Please, sir, don't tell that one," she says, gesturing towards Maurice. "Promise me you won't tell him."

"You have my word."

We ride on in silence.

"What's your name?" I ask after a while.

"My name is Aiyana," she replies. "It means endless beauty."

"That fits you well."

"Thank you. What is your name?" she asks.

"My name is Maximilian. You can call me Max."

"What does that mean?"

"Mean? I don't know. I suppose it means 'big.'"

She seems to blush.

"May I call you Lily?" I ask.

She looks perplexed.

"Why?"

"Because where I come from, if you like someone, you give them a special name. We call it a nickname. The name I will give you is Lily."

"What is Lily?"

"Lily's a beautiful flower."

"I am already beautiful. I'm Aiyana."

"To everyone else you're Aiyana. But to me you're Lily."

"Lily..." she says, turning away.

"Where are you from?" I ask her.

"I was born in Afghanistan", she says. "My father was an Afghani trader in precious gems. We moved to Mombasa when I was six. I worked in the shop every day."

"Didn't you go to school?" I ask.

"No. But in the shop, I learned the value of diamonds, rubies, emeralds, and sapphires. I saw that of all the gems, diamonds are the most powerful. More powerful than any currency. Diamonds can buy anything."

I look at her.

"What a coincidence," I tell her. "It so happens that I'm on a quest to find a treasure in lost diamonds."

"What lost diamonds?" she asks.

I tell her the story of why I'm in Africa.

"How did you come to be with the German?" I ask her.

"My father apprenticed me to a French colonial jewel merchant so I could learn to speak French and English. But he...he took advantage of me. I was twelve..."

She tenses and stops talking.

After a long moment looking into some distant place she continues, "When my father learned I'd been ruined, he sold me to Arab traders. It's hard to speak of that time... The Arabs sold me to a gang of German mercenaries. I never saw my family again..."

She breathes, pausing again to gather herself.

"The mercenaries made me their concubine..." she continues evenly. "Until I caught the eye of a tribal chief. Then I became the chief's fourth wife..."

Despite tormenting memories, her exquisitely beautiful face remains serene, signaling a woman of considerable courage and grit.

As I listen, I can't stop marveling at her extraordinary predicament.

"What was that like?" I venture, trying not to betray my alarm.

"The chief was cruel. When I tried to run away, he beat me. One day he came to my dogan drunk. When I refused to make love, he began to hit me, so I killed him with a long knife." She looks away, remembering. "The other wives embraced me with tears of joy. But I had to run away. That's how I came to be with the German. The German captured me and put me in chains."

She looks at me.

"The German was going to kill me. You saved my life."

"Anyone would have done the same."

"No. Most men would not have done the same," she says, nodding towards Maurice, who rides up ahead. "Men like him. He doesn't have a good heart. He would have let me die."

"You don't have to worry anymore," I say. "The German's dead. No one's going to hurt you now."

She takes a moment to weigh what I've said.

"What are you going to do with me?"

"It hasn't been decided."

"Are you going to sell me?"

"I can't say. What do *you* want?"

She looks puzzled.

"What do *I* want...? No one ever asked me that question."

"I'm asking you. What do you want?"

She doesn't answer.

Towards the end of the day, Maurice pulls up. "There's an oasis up ahead," he says. "We'll camp there."

11

We make camp in a patch of green in a sea of sand and parched earth. In the middle, a pool of cold spring water percolates up from an aquifer of ancient rain deep beneath the earth.

"What were you talking about with the woman?"

"She speaks French."

"You spoke French with her?"

"Yes."

"What did she say?"

"She wants to know if we're going to sell her."

We finish erecting the tent and build a small fire. I shoot a curious bush pig that carelessly wanders into the perimeter of firelight. We skewer the meat on a camp spit.

Attracted by the aroma, Lily emerges from her tent avoiding eye contact with Maurice. A quick glance sends me a message that it would be better if we were alone, better if we didn't have to playact for the Belgian. I cut meat off the spit and hand it to her. She retires to her tent to eat alone.

"You see how she behaves?" Maurice says, unaware of the interaction. "The culture gap is unbreachable. You should listen to me."

"I told you. I don't see a problem."

"Then you figure it out."

He's clearly impatient. But now there's a more ominous tone to his voice.

"I will."

We finish the meal and sip tea in silence, contemplating for a long time the night sky and the canopy of palms above flickering in light from the fire.

Maurice catches me off guard with another surprise.

"I once owned a slave myself," he says matter-of-factly, breaking the silence.

I turn, cup suspended in hand.

"That's right. I don't mind telling you. I had a slave. And I was even a slaver."

I stare at him for a long moment.

"Of course, you're joking."

"Not at all," he says. "I'm quite serious."

I put the cup on the ground, prepared to listen.

"How did that happen?"

He gathers his thoughts.

"It was back at the beginning of the war," he says. "Since I'd deserted, I couldn't go home. So after the incident in Congo, and before I got into the diamond business, I fell in with some mercenaries. We wound up in Mombasa, where some of us were recruited to go into the interior and round up slaves for the Arabs. Do you know it's Arabs who ran the slave trade? It was very lucrative, and I made a lot of money. I soon quit, but not before witnessing terrible things."

"What was the worst thing you ever saw?" I ask, fascinated by his confession.

"The worst thing I ever saw was the killing of women and children in one village. It was the work of one man. He acted alone. Shot seventeen women and children, even babies. The man who did this was none other than the German deserter and mercenary that you dispatched with our lady guest. Helmut Knauss. We did the world a favor killing him. I thought you might like to know."

"Small world. You owned a slave?"

"She became my wife."

"A slave wife? Where is she?" I ask.

"She was taken by the influenza pandemic of '18. I was very attached to her. I knew other men who took up with slave women, men too busy to bother with courtship and that sort of thing. For the most part, their stories have happy endings."

I find that hard to believe.

Can Lily possibly have a happy ending?

12

The next day, with waterbags refreshed once more to bursting and the horses rested, watered, and well fed, we mount up for the final push to Timbuktu.

Maurice rides alone.

But that evening as we're setting up camp, he turns to me and says: "Have you been talking to the woman?"

"Yes. She has a name. Her name is Aiyana."

"What kind of name is that?"

"It's Afghani. It means endless beauty."

He's noncommittal.

"Do you have a plan? We're running out of time."

"I'm working on it."

"Oh, good," he says sarcastically. "Just be sure to let me know when you finally make up your mind."

Late the following day, Timbuktu rises like a cluster of troglodyte castles, looming dark and sinister against an orange sky. We hear a strange wailing as we ride closer. It's the caterwauling of muezzins calling the faithful to prayer.

"I don't like the feel of this place," I say, sensing something like a chill in spite of the heat.

"It takes getting used to," Maurice replies.

The gates of the walled city swing open, and inside the streets are alive with Arab traders. A mixed funk of camel sweat and unwashed men hangs thick in the dusty, swirling air, a cacophony of shouting merchants crowded shoulder to shoulder. Above the bedlam, camels bellow, bemoaning their sorry lot. Bedouins, Tuaregs and Berbers intermingle in animated clusters, haggling and bartering with wildly theatrical gestures over trade goods and camels. There's a long-suffering dancing bear on a rope, a man selling doves in wicker cages, and the savory aroma of a goat roasting over an open pit. Drums beat and men dance like dervishes.

"I'd say it's a pretty good party. But where are the women?"

We position Lily between us, to protect her.

"Good luck finding any in this town," Maurice answers. "This is a man's world. That's why you'd better keep an eye on your lady friend, because she's sure to attract attention."

Heads are already turning to stare at the obviously female figure on the mule.

"Maybe if we're lucky somebody'll steal her," he says, enjoying a little private humor.

Soon, in the heart of the city, we pull up in front of a walled compound. As in Marrakesh, guards armed with rifles stand ready to greet us. They seem to be expecting our arrival and open the gates. In the entrance courtyard, a strikingly beautiful European woman, unusually tall and elegant, comes forward to welcome us. At her side is a magnificent cheetah on a gold chain. The woman stands straight as Aphrodite, garbed head to toe in a lustrous sapphire-blue jalaba, her eyes a matching brilliant sea blue. Her hair, shining full and uncovered in the Western fashion, is a lustrous dark blond.

I can understand Maurice's weakness.

We dismount.

The yellow-eyed cat appears to be staring at me with unusual interest.

"Max, I'd like to introduce you to Lady Edwina."

"Please, call me Edwina," she says, looking directly into my eyes, offering her hand. "This is Sawara," turning toward the cat. "Don't be alarmed. She's quite used to visitors. Hasn't eaten anyone in years!"

When we fail to laugh, Edwina glances over my shoulder.

"Just having a bit of fun," she says. "Who's this?"

"Her name is Aiyana. I call her Lily. We rescued her out of a bad situation."

"Well, I can see she's a very pretty girl."

I'm keeping an eye on the cheetah.

"You may pet her," Edwina says, coming closer. I smell an intoxicating perfume. "She likes people, and she loves to be touched."

The cheetah, motionless, locks on to me with an intensely feral gaze.

"Well, go on!" Edwina admonishes. "She won't bite!"

I reach out tentatively.

The cat bares its fangs and hisses.

"Or maybe she will," I say, quickly snatching back my hand.

Lily walks straight up to the cheetah and bends to cup the cat's head in her hands. For several moments, both make soft murmuring sounds.

"You see?" Edwina observes. "You just have to have the right touch. Sawara seems to have found a friend. I can always rely on her instincts."

Lily kisses the cheetah's face, then continues to stroke the cat.

"You can always trust a cheetah," Lily says. "I had one once when I was the wife of a king. But I loved the cheetah more than I loved the king. When I wanted privacy and protection, my cheetah slept with me."

She gives me an apologetic look, realizing she's blundered by speaking English. Maurice looks surprised but says nothing.

"I'm sure there's more to that story!" Edwina says, taking Lily by the arm. "But first you should rest. You've come a long way. I'll show you to your room."

To me she adds: "Sirhan will take you to your quarters. You'll have time to relax and bathe, if you wish. We'll have dinner in the garden at eight."

Inside, Maurice mutters to me accusingly: "You knew she spoke English. Why didn't you tell me?"

"She didn't want you to know. She's afraid of you. I can't say I blame her, given your behavior."

"Whose side are you on, anyway? She's a whore and a slave. And I almost forgot... a murderer too."

I ignore him and move on, following tall, turbaned Sirhan into the house.

What awaits behind massive wooden doors reminds me immediately of the surreal setting of our dinner at the Banker's. We walk into shimmering light from a thousand candles. It's a trompe l'oeil effect that rivals the great halls and grand palazzos of Europe. Candy for eyes dulled by days in the desert.

"Do you see how she played Edwina?" Maurice mutters. "This is just the beginning..."

I ignore the question.

"What is it with you people and your candles and mirrors?" I ask.

"It's all part of the show..."

"What show?"

He gives me a knowing look but doesn't answer.

As we advance further, the mystery of the house deepens.

"This place is huge. Where's the furniture?" I ask as we move from one carpeted room to another.

"Edwina lives the Arab way. Cushions, pillows, and carpets."

"Does she live alone?"

"It's a question I don't ask. Nor should you."

Moorish fountains scented by floating flowers move water through a network of channels along the base of the walls, making the air moist and cool.

"Check your boots for scorpions. And sometimes asps hide under the beds," Sirhan tells us when we finally arrive at our quarters. "Lady Edwina will see you at dinner."

My room is lighted by candles. The ceiling is tented. French doors open on a private garden bursting with wild roses and purple bougainvillea. In the corner, a fountain murmurs, sending a small gurgling cascade into a basin that releases water to circulate.

A quick look under the bed reveals no asps. I shake out a pair of babouches, Moorish slippers placed in the closet for guests. No scorpions. The bathroom is spacious, with a tub fit for a pharaoh. My bath has been drawn, the water scented and sprinkled with desert sage, a nice masculine touch amidst all the flowers and finery. Still trying to put it all together, I sink into the bath. But instead of blissful relaxation, my mind turns to irrational thoughts.

I imagine an intruder stabbing me to death in the tub, like Marat.

I think of Lily stabbing the king.

13

At dinner in the garden, we're directed to a table and chairs, where we await the arrival of our hostess. She appears presently in a long red jalaba, accompanied by a graceful figure clad only in white. It's not until she pulls back the cowl of her burnoose to reveal her face that we realize the person in white is none other than our Nefertiti, utterly transformed.

"Lily!" I exclaim happily, my admiration and surprise abundantly evident.

We take in the full measure of Lily's revealed persona. She's a Mesopotamian goddess with classic beauty to match the American Gibson Girls, or the radiant stars in Hollywood starting to light up the silver screen back home. Her skin is lustrous, her lips full. Her hair, shining silky black, falls loose and smooth to her shoulders.

Nefertiti in the flesh.

"The desert can take a terrible toll on all of us. I thought this lovely girl could use a little freshening up," Edwina says, looking proudly upon her creation.

She leads us to a spectacular dining pavilion illuminated by a galaxy of candles. A tented roof has been rolled back to reveal the stars.

"Now it's time to eat. You must be starving."

As plates of roast lamb and couscous appear, Edwina raises a glass in salute to Lily.

"A toast to our special guest."

Lily raises her glass. Uncertain, she watches carefully, imitating our behavior. Unfamiliar with forks and knives, she feeds herself with her fingers. An attendant steps forward, unfolds her napkin and places it in her lap.

"Lily and I have had a lovely time getting to know one another. She told me her story. Unfortunately, it's all too common in this part of the world."

"We've heard the Turks almost captured you, Edwina, and what a crack shot you are," I say.

"The secret is to maintain a steady hand but move with lightning speed, before your adversary can react or even understand what's happening," Edwina responds. "In altercations, it's one of the many benefits of being a woman. We have the advantage of surprise. And women are better shots. Did you know that? But my father made sure I could take care of myself from an early age."

Then, turning back to Lily, she announces with youthful enthusiasm:

"Lily's confided to me her most secret desire!"

Lily looks puzzled.

"What you want to do with your life?" Edwina prompts.

"Ah, yes," Lily says. "I want to learn how to fly."

"There!" Edwina cries triumphantly. "What do you think of that?"

She looks at us expectantly.

"You're going to teach her!" Edwina exclaims, looking at both of us. "You're very familiar with the Spad and I have access to one. I've been wanting to do a little flying myself, but pilots are in short supply. So while you're at it, you can give me a few lessons, too."

Edwina drains her wine.

"We'll all be pilots!" she says. "Now it's time to eat. You must be starving."

Plates of roast lamb and couscous appear. For the next few minutes the table goes silent as we focus on excellent food in abundant variety.

"Now to business..." Maurice says, breaking the silence and setting down his fork.

"Maurice, you should know better," Edwina scolds. "A gentleman never discusses business at table."

"In our world, as you well know, the table is often the *only place* where we discuss business, Lady Edwina. Particularly here in the desert."

"I'm aware of what you wish to discuss, and it will have to wait."

Maurice, rebuked, turns his attention back to the meal.

After dinner, Edwina leads us to a torch-lit, English-style gazebo with cushioned wicker chairs where brandy and cigars await.

"This is where we talk business," Edwina says pointedly, making herself comfortable. An attendant lights her cigar and pours brandy into snifters.

"The finest Havana," she says, blowing a thin wisp of blue smoke. "You won't find these in Africa. The brandy is Hardy Cognac Printemps. You won't find that in Africa, either. Except here in my castle."

Her demeanor's haughty, superior, every inch a queen of the desert.

Maurice and I light cigars and taste the brandy. I'm indifferent to the cigars and even less interested in the brandy. But Maurice adapts comfortably to the elegance, appearing to savor each sip, and drawing upon the cigar to casually blowing smoke rings toward the darkened heavens.

Lily watches everything with interest but says nothing.

"So you want to know about the missing diamonds?" Edwina begins, addressing Maurice. She holds her cigar off to the side, like a cigarette. "The only person in the world who can answer that question, of course, is El Gato."

"That's true only if El Gato himself has any knowledge of where Sehrgitz may have hidden his stash," Maurice replies, watching a smoke ring dissipate as it rises towards the stars. "The sum, a mere fifty million dollars or so, may not even be enough to get his attention. But it's enough to make a real difference to the victims of the crime and to the national economies of both Belgium and France. That's why I'm here."

"Oh stop the theatrics, Maurice!" she snaps dismissively. "I know precisely why you're here. You want to appropriate those missing diamonds for yourself. Of course, I can't say I blame you. It's a sizable sum."

"Wherever did you get that idea?" Maurice asks, blowing another smoke ring and studying his cigar.

"You can't fool me," she says, scarcely able to conceal her scorn. "And you'd bloody well better not try to fool yourself. We're all thieves, and you know it."

"I don't suppose it would do any good to refute all that?" he says, taking another sip of brandy.

"Save your breath. I prefer to have the cards on the table. It gives me peace of mind."

Now Edwina blows a perfect smoke ring, then another.

"This is not a singularly masculine talent," she says. "How do you like your cigars?"

"Very nice," Maurice says absently.

"And the brandy?"

"Excellent," I tell her.

I let the amber liquid warm in my mouth before swallowing.

"Where do you suppose we can find El Gato now?" I ask, feeling the sweet heat go down.

"You missed him by only a few weeks," she says, getting back to business. "He should be in Fucauma by now. But Fucauma is a very long way. You could go there only to find he's moved on. He does that. He disappears. Then where would you be? Maybe it'd be best to wait for him here. I'm expecting him in a month's time."

"Wouldn't that be an imposition?" I ask.

"Not at all. Actually, for Lily and me it could be an opportunity."

14

All's quiet early the next morning as Edwina, mounted on a fine black Arab, leads us clip-clopping along empty streets, then out through the city gates. Lily, elevated from consignment to mule, rides ahead alongside Edwina on a gentle mare. They're immersed in conversation.

Maurice and I take up the rear.

"It looks like Lily's found a friend."

"It would seem so," Maurice says. "Maybe the problem will solve itself."

"I was hoping to have some time with Lily myself."

"Be careful what you wish for," he says. "Out here, I'm telling you, solitary women can mean trouble."

"Men can be trouble, too. I've already had to kill two. And we have no idea where El Gato's hiding. As for women, I think Lily's an asset."

"All we know for certain is that she's a fugitive and a wanted murderer," he says.

"We also know she's beautiful and intelligent."

"There's more to her than meets the eye. I'll wager she's not what you think."

"Is that so? Then what is she, do you think?"

"She's a killer."

"How would you know?"

"I can smell it."

I almost laugh. "She doesn't even own a gun."

"Edwina's teaching her to shoot."

"I don't know why that should worry you."

"You're naïve, Max. You accept things at face value. But I can see right through that girl."

His endless harping has become a constant annoyance.

"Maybe you read too much into things, Maurice," I tell him, scarcely able to hide my impatience. "And you needn't worry about me. I can take care of myself."

Up ahead, Lily suddenly reins in her horse. Edwina pauses to watch as Lily dismounts and walks over to where a child lies sleeping by the side of the road. A few feet away, a woman crouches against a wall, her face buried in her knees.

Maurice and Edwina move on together while I move up to hold Lily's horse.

Lily kneels, brings the listless child up into her arms, and gently rocks it back and forth. The woman lifts her head. Tears streak the black lining under her eyes. She says something. They have a conversation. Lily puts down the child, hands something to the woman, and walks back to her horse.

She has tears in her eyes.

"What's going on?" I ask.

"That little girl starved to death today. When I was a child in Afghanistan, I saw lots of children die. Even some of my friends. I gave the mother all the bread I have."

I'm speechless. All I can do is nod.

She gets back on her horse and we move forward in silence.

An hour later at the aerodrome the sun's already a furnace. A detachment of French Foreign Legionnaires waves us through a barbed wire perimeter and into the welcome shade of a large field tent with side flaps open to circulate hot air and capture whatever slight breeze might come our way.

"Madame Edwina!" the Commandant salutes smartly. "Bienvenu. Comment puis-je vous aider?"

Welcome. How may I help you?

"It never fails to amaze me, Captain, how you survive in such heat," Edwina replies in French. "It must take a very special type of man."

"You're too kind, ma'am. We all do our duty. We'll remain here and protect the field as long as required. There's talk of air service between Casablanca and Timbuktu."

"Yes, I know. The man behind the plan was kind enough to provide me the Spad which is in your care. Now could you please bring us water and take us to my plane?"

"Immediately!" At his gesture, an orderly appears with large field cups brimming with cool water from the oasis spring.

Still standing, we drain our cups.

"Thank you," Edwina says, handing hers to an orderly. "I feel like a new woman."

"Would you like to see your Spad?"

"Lead on!"

We cross open scrabble to the edge of the oasis.

"There she is," the Captain says.

We peer into the foliage but see nothing that resembles an aeroplane. I squint against the glare, trying to make out an outline of a Spad concealed somewhere among the shadows of greenery, but there's nothing.

"Are my eyes playing tricks on me in this frightful heat?" Edwina asks. "I see no plane."

"Voila!" the Captain says.

With that, several legionnaires pull away palm fronds to reveal a military camouflage net. When they peel back the net, we're greeted by the most beautiful flying machine I've ever seen, a fire-engine red, two-seat Spad XV1, crouching as if poised to leap into the air like a giant scarlet dragonfly.

"How lovely she is!" Edwina exclaims.

"Has she ever been flown?" I ask.

"She flew missions during the war," the Captain says. "She wasn't so pretty then."

We turn to Lily, who's totally absorbed. I realize she's probably never seen a flying machine before.

"What do you think?"

"I want to learn to fly this amazing bird," she says.

"And so you shall," Edwina says. "So shall we all! When can we start?"

"Max and I will take her up and check her out." Maurice says. He turns to the Captain: "Fuel?"

"Enough war surplus to last a year. Plus a few truckloads we confiscated from some Germans nearby. And that's not to mention enough to start an air service we're getting from an unnamed commercial enterprise in Spanish Sahara. The Spad is full. She may never be empty."

As senior pilot, Maurice climbs into the rear seat while I stand by at the varnished wooden propellor. When he shouts "contact!" I pull the prop down hard with both hands. The engine sputters, coughs, belches blue exhaust and begins to rumble. I clamber aboard, sliding into the front. The Spad shudders like a chained beast straining to be free.

The engine growls as we taxi out onto a dirt strip, then roars. We bump down the runway, picking up speed. Suddenly, smoothly, we're airborne, climbing effortlessly into a cloudless sky. The plains of Africa fall away and stretch to an infinite dun-colored horizon. At six thousand feet the air cools. Maurice rolls the Spad onto her back and we dive into a loop-de-loop, swooping down in a wild rush, engine screaming, then back up, heavy with G-forces. Now we're standing on our tail. When the Spad stalls, Maurice lets it fall over backwards and flips it into a tailspin. We level off at three thousand feet and enjoy a leisurely return to earth.

For all my reservations about Maurice, I can't deny he's a good pilot.

"I was certain you were both going to die," Edwina shouts as we pull up.

"She's solid," Maurice calls back. "She performs beautifully."

"I've been learning to fly this sort of plane, thanks to my friends in the French Foreign Legion," Edwina says.

"Why didn't you tell me?" Maurice asks.

"I love surprise, don't you?" Edwina says. "Let me show you what I can do!"

Moments later, Edwina is roaring down the strip. She climbs into the sky, swings around, then dives back down like a bird of prey, swooping just yards over our heads. She makes another low pass, then lands.

She taxis over and cuts the engine.

"That was impressive," Maurice says.

"Thank you." Edwina turns to Lily. "Your turn!"

Lily approaches the Spad and runs her hands over the plane's shiny red skin.

"You're all like gods," she says. "Now I, too, will become a god."

"You may never be a god," I tell her. "But you may be one of the only women in Africa who can fly."

"Teach me," she teases. "I'll be better than you!"

I help her mount the wing and negotiate her and her flowing jalaba, a considerable nuisance, into the confined space of the passenger cockpit.

"We need to get you flying clothes," I tell her.

"I'm nervous!" she says.

"Just relax. You're safe with me."

Maurice cranks the prop. We taxi, rush down the runway and lift off, climbing to five hundred feet, then cruise in leisurely circles.

"Tomorrow we'll do takeoffs and landings," I tell her after we land.

We ride back to the sanctuary in suffocating heat. The horizon, distorted by mirages, seems to tremble. The horses sweat and froth. No one speaks. Behind the thick walls of the compound, the temperature's a refreshing thirty degrees cooler. Edwina and Lily disappear to the women's quarters while Maurice and I seek rehydration on an arbored terrace bordering a shallow wading pool the length of a bocce court. A marble statue of a urinating Eros dominates the far end. We settle into wicker chairs. An attendant appears almost immediately with minted lemon iced tea.

"So what do you think?" I ask, keeping it cordial, settling back glass in hand.

He launches right in.

"You know what I think. I think we should have gotten rid of that bitch while we had a chance. She's ingratiating herself with Edwina and she's obviously got you wrapped around her little finger, as well. I promise you, she's going to be nothing but trouble."

I take a moment.

"Look, this is getting tiresome. You don't know what you're talking about. You're obsessed with her, yet you hardly know her. Maybe if you showed her a little respect, you'd see what I see."

"Respect? She's a primitive tribal girl who grew up in black Africa. You'll find out the hard way I was right all along."

"Why do you feel so threatened? I'll bet you were one of those kids who saw a monster under every bed."

He scoffs.

"The only monster I see is a Medusa. And she'll make trouble. Mark my words."

15

We're at the aerodrome the following morning in time to beat the worst of the heat. Lily, decked out in one of Edwina's flying outfits, bounces the Spad down the strip on her first takeoff attempt, which I have to abort. But on her third try we lift off smoothly and climb steadily into cooler air.

"I did it!" she shouts to me over her shoulder.

The landing's problematic. We go around several times. But on the fourth attempt, she brings the Spad down without incident, and we roll to the end of the runway.

"I'm now a pilot!" she calls to a smiling Edwina, who claps her hands.

"No, Lily," I kiss her cheek. "You're not a pilot until you're able to fly alone – solo."

She gives me a pouty look.

While Maurice and Edwina go back up in the Spad, Lily and I sit on field chairs in the shade of the palms and watch the performance overhead.

"I've been thinking..." she says after a minute.

"About flying?"

"About everything," she says.

"How so?"

She frowns.

"Some things you don't have to explain," she says, and shifts her gaze back to the heavens.

"Look at that. It's magic."

The Spad's making figure eights, a red fleck wheeling in the blue. The far-off drone of her engine is like the hum of a distant bumblebee, the only sound in the vastness of desert and sky.

"For the first time in my life, I'm not sad," she says, still looking up.

"Are you happy?"

"If you're no longer sad, then you're happy, no? You saved my life, Max. And now you teach me how to fly like a bird, how to be a god."

"I'll help you any way I can, Lily...I want to protect you and make sure you're happy."

"Thank you, Max. Is that love?"

"I don't know. But it must be close to that. Have you ever been in love?" I ask.

She shakes her head, no.

"Have you?"

"Yes," I say, remembering. "She was sixteen. I was fourteen. I felt like I'd been hit by a truck. But she wouldn't give me the time of day."

"Why not?"

"Because I was too young for her. To teenagers two years is a lifetime."

"Do you still love her?"

"No, of course not. But I still think about her sometimes. I've dated a lot of girls since then."

"Are you dating me, Max?"

I laugh.

"I'm definitely dating you, Lily."

"Can you teach me to love?" she asks.

"Nobody can teach love. But you'll know it when it happens."

"I want to love you, Max... I just need time..."

"I have all the time in the world. As long as it takes."

"When I fall in love how will I know?"

"Because it will be unlike anything you've ever known."

She grips my hand.

"But first I need to find myself," she says, the grip tightening. "I don't even know who I am."

My eyes trace the path of the Spad, carving lazy circles in the sky.

"I don't know who I am, either" I tell her. "I'm not even supposed to be here."

"Where are you supposed to be?"

I tell her about Wall Street.

"A street with a wall in America? I have never heard of this place."

"You're not missing much."

"I'm glad you're not at your Wall Street."

We sit quietly for a moment.

Presently, I ask: "What do you want, Lily?"

"I just want to live...What do you want?"

I turn to her.

"What if I said I want you?"

She gives me a long, questioning look.

"I wouldn't believe you..."

"Why not?"

"Because we're very different."

"Is that bad?"

"It's not easy..."

"It doesn't have to be hard..."

"But it is, Max. What do you want me for? Do you want me to be your slave?"

"No! Why would you say that?"

"It is permitted."

"I would never want you to be my slave."

"Then... what for?"

"I want you just as you are, Lily. Not 'for' anything. Free do as you please."

"I've never been free, Max. Are you free? I don't even know what that means."

"I will show you. With me you'll always be free."

"Don't you have wives?"

"No. But if I did, where I come from, you're only allowed one."

"My father once had many wives," she says. "How can a man live with only one wife?"

"In America, many men think one wife is too many."

She laughs.

Then she turns to look at me. Her fingers touch my arm. Her eyes are soft and loving.

"You're the only man who's ever been good to me, Max," she says. "The only man I've ever known who didn't hurt me. You're not like Maurice."

"Did Maurice hurt you?"

"I'm afraid of him. He's like the others. From the beginning, I have not trusted him."

"Did he abuse you?" I ask again.

She glances away.

"Lily?"

"The Belgian is not who you think he is," she says after a pause. "He is not your friend. He will betray you. He came to my tent. I sent him away."

"He came to your tent?"

She looks away.

"Don't worry, Lily," I tell her. "Nothing's going to happen to you."

"No, Max. You don't understand. I'm afraid he'll kill me. The last time, when I told him I will never let him have his way with me, he called me a bitch and slapped me. I slapped him back and he threw me to the ground. He said if I ever try to resist him again, he will kill me."

I let it sink in, choking off the rage.

Edwina lands the plane and taxis to a stop. She and Maurice climb down and approach.

"Well, that was a great success," she announces. "Tonight's the full moon. We're going to celebrate! You gentlemen might want to spruce up."

As we ride back to the compound, I pull ahead to join Edwina and Lily, leaving Maurice to ride alone. Moments later, he gallops past, and disappears into the desert.

That night, we meet for a late dinner under a full Saharan moon. Edwina, Queen of the Desert, makes a spectacular entrance, looking every inch like a real queen in a green kaftan, complemented by a glittering diamond choker. Lily, the trader's daughter, is done up like European royalty. She's wrapped in an ivory silk gown that seems to glow in the candlelight. A fat diamond the size of a quail's egg set in sapphires hangs on her neck. The diamond flashes with every breath she takes.

"We thought we'd dress specially," Edwina says, sweeping out onto the terrace. "Tonight we celebrate the full moon and the wonderful new world of human flight, and of course our honored guest, Lily. What do you think of her?"

"Stunning."

"Where's Maurice?"

"I've not seen him."

"Very bad manners," Edwina says, clearly displeased.

We take our places at an al fresco dining table illuminated by candlelight.

"We have a special dish tonight, a delicacy of the desert," Edwina announces as attendants pour wine all around.

On her cue, the servants place a platter in the center of the table. In the middle of the platter, crowned in olive leaves, is the cooked head of a lamb on a bed of chickpeas, garlic and herbs.

"Lahem Ras. A favorite dish throughout the Arab world, especially Morocco. Fasi introduced me to it," Edwina explains. "The cheek and tongue are the most tender. Tonight we will dine with our fingers in the traditional way."

I seem to be the only one unfamiliar with this local favorite. The sheep appears to be smiling. The eyes stare back at me. Edwina's the first to rip a bite-sized morsel off the cheek and slip it into her mouth, followed immediately by Lily, who does the same. In moments, we're all pulling at the head.

By the time I get my hand in, most of both cheeks are gone. But I still find a nice piece. To my surprise, it's remarkably savory. The next portion is a piece of the tongue, which requires strategic manipulation with a small knife. Taking part of the tongue while the animal is looking at me takes getting used to.

Lily smiles. She's obviously enjoying herself.

"I thought you might like it," Edwina says. "I was thinking of you."

"When I was a girl, we used to have Lahem Ras on special occasions," Lily says. "Once I got used to it..."

"I want you to feel at home here, Lily," Edwina says, reaching out to touch her hand. "No harm will come to you here."

After dinner, I take Lily aside.

"Will you walk with me?"

We step out under a glittering carpet of stars.

I take her hand. The electricity between us is tangible.

Everything else seems to melt away.

In the middle of the garden, I stop to face her.

The image of Nefertiti gazing across time in the moonlight is achingly beautiful.

"Now that we're alone... I want to tell you..."

I pause, feeling a powerful pulse of heat in my chest.

"Lily... I love you..."

The words are out. I've said it.

She looks into my eyes for a long moment.

Then, wordlessly, she moves closer and wraps her arms around me, clinging fiercely. We stay that way for several minutes, motionless in magical moonglow, listening to endless silences.

"I want to marry you," I tell her.

I feel her grip tighten.

"But Max, you don't even know me..." she whispers.

"I know what I see. I see a beautiful woman, inside and out. I see somebody I could spend the rest of my life with..."

I feel her body let go. She begins to tremble. I feel tears through my shirt.

"I'm just a slave girl... shamed and humiliated... I'm unworthy..."

She's sobbing now, tears running hot, pressing her face against my chest. Her body smells sweet, like the flowers in the garden.

"No woman in my eyes was ever more worthy, Lily...No woman was ever more beautiful...," I tell her gently. "You'll never be a slave again..."

She pulls back, her face wet with tears.

"Max," she says, her voice unsteady, barely able to speak. "No man... has ever said these words to me..."

We gaze into each other's eyes so deeply, the rest of the world seems to fall away, leaving us suspended in time and space.

"Come," she whispers after a while, taking me by the hand. She leads me through the moonlight past fountains and gazebos, to a small bathing pool nestled in the corner of her private residence. The sweet scents of wild roses and night-blooming jasmine fill the air.

"Here," she says. She drops her jalaba, and naked, enters the water, turning to face me.

The full-flowered beauty of her body takes my breath away.

I cast my clothes aside and step into the water.

She puts her hand to my chest.

"Slowly, Max," she whispers. "Please. Slowly..."

I put my hands on her arms.

Her arms stiffen.

"I don't know how to do this," she murmurs. "It's never been like this for me..."

"I love you, Lily" is all I can say.

Her eyes behold mine in a look of wonder.

"Every time you say that I can't believe it..."

"Believe it. I love you, Lily..."

She inches forward uncertainly. Time seems to slow. Each tiny movement is excruciatingly, painstakingly, an act of unconditional love. Our mouths barely touch, the delicate kiss lingering for a long minute.

I feel welcoming warmth and soft ripeness in her lips, detect tantalizing hints of body musk in the smoothness of her skin.

"Yes, like that, Max," she whispers, pressing closer now.

"Yes...just like that...gently..."

The kiss becomes more urgent as she wraps her arms, then her legs, around me. Now we're one, fused together, inseparable, in an eager embrace more powerful than anything I've ever known. The heat of her skin, the musky scent, low, catlike resonance of her voice, even the wild beating of our hearts all converge like a wave as she thrusts up and takes me inside her.

The wave sweeps me to another place. Strange animal-like sounds that I've never heard erupt from deep within both of us, as if we were locked in some desperate, mortal combat from which no one can survive.

After, we share a long and loving kiss. Our lips linger, reluctant to part, until she says:

"I must go."

She floats away in silence, wrapping her jalaba around her, and disappears into her quarters. Sated and happy, I let myself sink underwater, floating weightless, marveling at how the last moments of day illuminate and sanctify the space around me like a divine light.

16

Ensuing days unfold with deceptive normality, with visits to the aerodrome, and more uneventful dinners under the stars. We're settling into a routine. But Lily and I share a secret. Maurice has completely disappeared, and Edwina seems inexplicably agitated. She snaps at the staff, struts up and down empty corridors as if looking for something or someone, rides off into the desert for hours at a time, and keeps conversations short -- all the while maintaining a mask of cordiality.

Once I catch her apparently having an animated conversation with herself by a window overlooking one of the gardens.

"Aha! Precisely!" I hear her saying. "Precisely! He must go. He must go. But we must be clever. Must never show our hand..."

I wonder if she might be talking to someone in the garden, but there's no one.

Then one night after dinner, Edwina announces she's off for a moonlight ride on her favorite Arab, a handsome, wild-eyed black stallion she says quivers with excitement every time he sees her.

She invites us to walk with her out to the stables.

"Your American cowboys think they have special relationships with their ponies?" she says. "Believe me, it can't compare to the bond between a woman and her stallion!"

There's a strange sound.

"There! You hear that?"

We all stop to listen.

A loud whinnying suddenly emanates from somewhere deep inside the moonlit stables, some fifty yards distant.

"He can sense my presence even before he sees me or hears me! That's what I'm talking about."

When we arrive at the stall, the horse is rearing and prancing and snorting with excitement.

Edwina's eyes glow with admiration.

"Can you see how happy he is to see me?"

She opens the gate and the animal bolts from the stall, almost knocking us over, and gallops out of the stables and into the moonlight.

"Have you ever in your life seen a more beautiful thing than that?" she asks, her face filled with adoration and awe.

"Alhuru!" she cries out. "Alhuru! Come to me!"

The horse charges straight back into the stable and pulls up short of where we're standing.

"Behold the unique and magnificent Alhura!" she declares grandly. "Look at him! What a splendid beast! There's not a finer horse in all the Arab world!"

"What does the name mean?" I ask.

"It means 'heat', which I equate with the power of the sun," she answers. "His sister, Luna, is my other favorite. I equate her with the power of the moon."

The horse rears and whinnies.

"You see that? All he wants is to become one with me and ride into the night! I won't disappoint!"

At that, Edwina takes off all her clothes.

Stunned, I feel an obligation to turn away. But I can't bring myself to stop watching. I continue to watch until she's totally naked.

I glance at Lily, who's equally amazed, but clearly making a mental note of my reactions. I hope my face doesn't betray my appreciation of Edwina's fine body.

"I'll need a hand to mount him," Edwina says, speaking directly to me.

"No saddle? No reins?"

"Of course not," she says. "That'd ruin everything."

"But how?"

"Don't you worry!" she admonishes. "Alhura knows precisely what to do. Just cup your hands so I can step up."

I make a cradle with my hands. She puts in her left foot, and I hoist her. Halfway, she slows just enough so that her buttocks and lavender-scented crotch make intimate contact with my face. I hardly have time to react. The next thing I know she's letting out a triumphant banshee shriek. Then she and Alhura thunder out of the stables and into the silver night, leaving Lily and me gaping at each other and marveling at what had just happened.

"I don't know what that was all about, or what she was trying to do," I tell Lily as we make our way back to the main house.

"I know what she was trying to do, Max," Lily says. "She was trying to shock us."

"Well, she succeeded..."

"She's crazy, Max. I could see she was enjoying it. Did you know you had an erection?"

I lead her to my quarters.

Without a word, we strip and sink onto the bed, two ghosts writhing in a wash of moonlight filtered through sheer curtains undulating in the night breeze.

After, I lie awoke and hold her in my arms, her head on my chest, until she stirs.

"Where are you going?"

"I must go back."

"Why?"

"Edwina made me promise not to leave the women's quarters at night."

"You're with me now. And she's running around naked on a horse somewhere in the desert."

"She says it's not safe."

"Maurice attacked you in the women's quarters. You're safer here with me."

"There are eunuch guards now. They have instructions to find me if I'm not in my quarters when I should be. They'll come looking for me."

"That sounds like a prison."

"She says she wants to protect me."

"From what? What's she afraid of?"

"She wants to control me. Maybe she thinks I'll run away."

"Why would you run away? Where would you go?"

"I wasn't going to tell you. Max. But she watches me all the time. Sometimes I think she follows me when she thinks I don't see her. But I see her hide. I think she may be obsessed with me."

"Why didn't you tell me?"

"Because I didn't want to upset you."

"It upsets me more when you don't tell me. Is there anything else?"

She gets up and walks to the window, looking into the silvery night. The moon has transformed everything to platinum, pearl and alabaster.

"When she teaches me to shoot, she always wraps her arms around me. She brushes against me and touches me. It makes me uncomfortable. I don't complain, because I'm grateful. I don't want to offend her, and I want to learn."

"Jesus. We've got to get out of here."

"I know."

17

Two nights later, well after midnight, I lie awake unable to sleep, tormented by strange visions and nervous energy I can't control. Drawn by the power of the moon and restless as a wild animal, I wander naked out on the terrace to gaze at the stars. There's no sound save the rustle of palms.

I sense her before I see her.

Turning, I see a surreal figure of a woman glowing like polished alabaster in the moonlight.

My god.

It's Edwina, golden hair cascading to her nipples. She looks no older than a schoolgirl fresh out of puberty.

She puts a finger to her lips.

Am I dreaming?

What's she doing?

Am I bewitched?

My conscience screams in protest.

I steel myself, knowing I've got to resist. But whatever righteous resolve I muster is no match for the overwhelming power that draws me inexorably to her and robs me of my will.

All thoughts of Lily are abandoned.

Edwina moves toward me in total silence, so close now I can smell heady lavender and feel her savage heat.

She reaches for me. The minute our fingers touch, I capitulate, as if struck by some kind of spell.

Shamelessly, my hands explore her body. Her hands explore mine. Our breathing becomes urgent, heavy.

She leads me through empty rooms to her candlelit bedchamber scented with roses.

She takes me by the hand, this beautiful woman old enough to be my mother, and draws me down upon her bed, welcoming me with a shared surge of animal passion that transports me to another world.

"Sawara likes to watch," she purrs in my ear.

I hadn't noticed the cheetah curled on a satin pillow in the corner of the room.

Later, when she finally drifts off to sleep, I sneak away, cursing myself, riddled with guilt and remorse. I navigate a lonely passage back through moonlit corridors, drained, dazed, and dissipated.

When I wake up in the morning in my own bed, the memory, vivid but elusive as an ebbing dream, rolls into my mind like the motion of the sea. Troubled and conflicted, I ask myself, Was I perhaps under the spell of some kind of exotic desert fever, a sleep-walking reverie brought on by the darker mysteries of the Saharan wilderness? Or perhaps some kind of hallucinatory stimulant in the food or wine?

Or was it seeing Edwina naked in the stables?

I find Lily and Edwina huddling together on the garden terrace. When Edwina spots me, she shows no recognition that anything out of the ordinary has occurred.

"Maximillian, come here!" she shouts, waving me over.

Closer, all thoughts of Edwina the night before are eclipsed by the shocking sight of Lily's left eye half shut.

There's ugly bruising and swelling.

"She's been attacked!" Edwina declares.

"What?"

"Maurice..." Edwina says.

Lily looks away.

"Lily?" I touch her arm. "What did he do?"

"He tried to rape her again," Edwina says. "I heard her scream and raced to her rescue. When Maurice saw me, he ran off into the night."

I feel a hot flush of fury.

"When I resisted, he hit me and held me by the throat," Lily says. "I thought he was going to strangle me...."

Ashamed and fighting tears, she excuses herself and hurries away.

I'm about to bolt after her when Edwina grabs my arm.

"Let her go," she says. "I'll see to her. And we'll deal with Maurice later. I've been teaching Lily how to shoot. Maybe Maurice will meet with a surprise if he tries again. Tomorrow will be an excellent opportunity to test her skills. Bush pigs. We'll be sure to bring her along. How about you, Max?"

Very matter of fact.

My mind's still reeling in the aftermath of Lily's stunning revelation, and my urge to rush off and comfort her. I struggle to keep it together and remain calm.

"Count me in."

There's a pause. I wait expectantly for any acknowledgment of the night before.

There's nothing but an awkward pause.

Finally, I establish full, unblinking eye contact.

"Tell me," I ask pointedly, "how was your evening?"

Gazing confidently into my eyes, Edwina reaches over and touches my groin.

"Very satisfactory... that is, before this unfortunate business with Lily." she says, smiling. "I like you, Max. You're up and coming. Maurice is out of control. I think it's time you and I got to know each other better."

18

Maurice reappears the next day just as we're mounting up to depart for the bush hunt.

"Where have you been?" Edwina snaps indignantly, her voice laced with wrath.

He ignores the question.

"We're going to shoot wild boar."

"I could use some water."

A houseman produces a goatskin. Maurice pours water on his face and head, takes a drink, then hangs the bag on his saddle.

We follow Edwina and Lily out of the compound, through the streets to the city gates and into the desert.

I let Maurice go on ahead, then wait until we're beyond the walls of the city to ride up and confront him.

"What did you do to Lily?"

"I don't know what you're talking about."

"She's upset."

"She's always upset."

"She says you were in her room last night and tried to rape her. She's got a black eye to prove it."

He looks away.

"She's a liar. Maybe she fell down and bumped her head."

"And Edwina caught you red-handed. If you touch her again I'll kill you,"

"I told you she'd be trouble!" he shouts as I ride off. "Do you believe me now?"

Moments later, the trackers gallop up and point to the southeast.

We divert and follow, stopping at a copse of dense, hardscrabble scrub. The trackers split, going in different directions.

"Prepare your guns," Edwina says, drawing her hunting rifle from her saddle. "The trackers will flush the boars from the thicket. We need to give the pigs space so they don't spook the horses or attack their guts. It will be fast. So be ready."

She and Lily, rifles at the ready, move off to the left. Maurice and I spread out to the right, leaving a narrow corridor.

Just then a herd of seven pigs bursts from cover, racing in our direction. Before they can get five meters, they're cut down in a deafening fusillade of gunfire. One, wounded, hobbles in a circle. Another, hit broadside, lies on its side, churning the air with its legs.

Edwina dismounts, walks over and shoots both dead with two quick pistol shots.

We can hear the trackers, drums louder, advancing closer through the bush. Edwina gets back on her horse.

"More coming!" she shouts, wheeling around, just as three big males burst out of the bush. She reaches for her rifle and retrieves it, but not before the alpha boar, a raging giant with huge tusks, makes straight for the underbelly of her Arab. Edwina pivots and gets off a wild shot, but the boar closes the distance in a flash, driving its tusks up into the horse's gut. The Arab moans and falters, then collapses on its side, taking Edwina down with it. Her leg is trapped under the stricken horse's disemboweled body. A pool of dark blood begins to spread immediately all around her.

Maurice and I get off a blast of simultaneous shots at the infuriated beast, hitting it in the abdomen and thigh. But incredibly, it doesn't go down. It's the third shot, delivered by Lily of the steady hand, that hits the pig squarely in the head, dropping it dead.

Suddenly, Lily aims her pistol at Maurice and pretends to fire.

"Bang! Bang!" she shouts, then raises her pistol fires a shot into the air.

Maurice, not amused, cries out, "Bloody fuck!"

"Oh! I mistook you for a pig!" Lily shouts.

I muscle Edwina out from under her fallen horse.

"I'm all right," she says, coming to her feet, testing her leg and leaning on me. "No broken bones. A bit sore but I'll be fine. Max, I'll ride with you. I need a bit of help."

There's a sorrowful animal groan.

"Oh my dear, dear Luna!" Edwina exclaims, anguished, turning her attention to her dying horse. She limps to the horse's head and kneels. "My dear, beloved Luna...What have they done to you?"

The Arab makes another strange sound. A big brown eye watches Edwina, who touches the horse's face, then gently moves her hand down to close the eye.

"Be still, my darling," she whispers, stroking the horse's cheek gently. "You've been my trusted friend, and I've loved you. Now it's time, my darling, to go to sleep..."

Then she takes out her pistol and shoots the horse in the middle of the forehead. The bang sends a shock wave through us all.

"Please help me up," Edwina says after a moment, returning her pistol to her holster. She glances down, sees she's drenched in blackening horse blood, drying fast in the sun.

"Take me home," she says, her voice weary.

"Ride with me, Edwina," Maurice calls out.

"Come, Max," she says, ignoring Maurice. "It's time we go."

At a signal from Edwina, the trackers salvage the saddle and tack from her fallen horse, then secure the smaller boars to their saddles. The big one, the size of a small pony, they drag on skids lashed to the horses.

"Thanks, but I must do this myself," Edwina admonishes, as I try to help her mount my horse. With difficulty, she pulls herself up and settles into the saddle behind me. She wraps her arms around my waist and rests her head on my shoulder.

On the ride back to the compound, Maurice comes alongside Lily and says something. They exchange a brief volley of words and she promptly pulls ahead, leaving him alone.

I turn to see him fall back, then gallop away.

When the compound gates swing open, Edwina lifts her head from my shoulder.

"El Gato..."

"Where?"

"The flag ..."

I glance up and see a pennant hanging on a pole.

"The coat of arms of the Noronha family," Edwina explains. "He's here."

I look back. Maurice is nowhere in sight.

Inside, Edwina lets me help her through the empty corridors, stopping at the door to her private chambers.

"Thank you," she says, lingering for a moment and turning to find my lips. The kiss is tender, unhurried, bold, and open-eyed.

Then she slips inside and closes the door.

Again, I feel a pang of self-loathing.

Not five minutes later, Lily, totally unaware, finds me and takes me aside. She leads me into an arbored portico with a small fountain and a bench.

"We've got to get out of this place, before we become crazy like these people" she whispers, gripping my arm. "They're both insane. Maurice just threatened me again. He says he won't stop until I give him what he wants. He thinks you're trying to take his place. And I know he wants to hurt you. And he says Edwina wants to seduce you so she can control you."

"What else did he say about Edwina?"

"He says she casts spells like a witch. She seduces every man who washes up here. Then she casts them aside or bends them to her will. Even worse, she's trying to have her way with me, too."

"Have her way with *you*?"

"There's so much you don't know. Look at this place!" she says, glancing around nervously. "It looks like paradise. But it's evil. It has a dark soul. Don't you feel it?"

"Don't worry," I say. "I promise I'll get us out of here."

"You have a plan?"

"Yes. A plan for us."

"What?"

"I'm going to take you to America."

Her eyes open wide.

'You'll never have to fear anybody again, Lily. You'll never have to want. In fact, you'll never have to want for anything as long as you live."

She has trouble putting her words together.

"But Max...," she begins, tears welling up. Why would you do that... for me?"

She looks at me in disbelief.

"Because I see you for what you are, Lily."

She pulls me close and wraps her arms around me.

"My only wish is to make you happy and give you the life you always deserved."

19

The following morning Edwina reemerges from seclusion a new woman. She finds me alone, eating papaya and scones on the terrace. There's no limp, no indication whatsoever she'd been drenched in blood and almost crushed.

The cheetah trots along beside her.

"You clean up well," I say, standing. "How do you feel?"

"Never better."

She takes a seat as a servant steps forward to pour juice.

The cheetah settles back on its haunches and never takes its yellow eyes off me,

"Where's El Gato?" I ask.

"He's gone off into the desert. He likes to be alone."

"Very strange," I say. "In fact, this whole place is strange. Maurice is a danger to Lily."

"I can handle Maurice."

"She fears for her life. She says you're scaring her, too."

"Whatever do you mean?"

"You know exactly what I mean, Edwina," I say, not holding back. "You're exploiting a vulnerable girl. This place is a nightmare. And you're part of the problem. We can't stay."

She seems to have heard nothing, almost as if she'd been expecting my outburst.

"Oh, you'll get used to it. Everybody does," she says dismissively, having a bite of a scone and getting comfortable.

"I don't plan to get used to it."

"Oh?" she says. "Are you planning to leave?"

"I was brought here under false pretenses. You're exploiting me and you're abusing Lily. I've got to get back, and I'm taking Lily with me."

"Dear boy, there's nothing for you to get back to."

"There's nothing for me here, Edwina."

"I'm here for you, Max. And this is where you'll make your fortune."

"Is this your way of offering me a job?"

"I'm offering you a new life."

"Explain to me why I would want to be part of a criminal organization."

She stiffens and draws back.

"Oh, please," she scoffs. "Let's be frank. For one thing, you're a fugitive and a murderer. Your options are limited."

I let that sink in.

The lines are drawn.

"It was a fine night, Edwina. But it's not enough to keep me here."

I see an indignant flash of anger.

"It disappoints me to hear you say that Max," she says, her voice edged with undisguised venom. "Just now when we're getting to know one another. This is all becoming very tiresome!"

At that, her eyes seem to morph into the eyes of a predatory cat.

I'm speechless, spellbound by the transformation.

Unconsciously, my hand inches toward my holster.

But then, just as suddenly, she seems to shape-shift right before my eyes back to seductive Siren from menacing Medusa.

Her eyes soften.

"What's come over you, sweet boy?" she purrs, her voice honied and sexy. "Has that little trickster Miss Lily been talking to you?"

"Lily and I have no secrets."

"Don't let yourself be fooled by that girl!" she comes right back. "I don't know what she's up to. But she's got an agenda."

"What kind of agenda?"

"She's completely delusional. She thinks she can find a better place. Can you imagine? After the life she's led and all I've done for her?"

I give it a moment.

"If you think you can incarcerate both of us here, *you're* delusional, Edwina."

That seems to rekindle the indignation.

"Unfortunately, Max, you've nowhere to go," she says, voice smooth, keeping it calm and moving closer. I sense the electric energy, feel myself getting sucked back into the familiar magic spell. Her sultry lidded eyes drop coyly to examine my lips.

For an instant I think she's going to kiss me.

"It's I who make the decisions here, my darling" she says, almost whispering. Her forefinger touches my mouth.

The cheetah hisses, drawing her attention. She produces a brick-size chunk of raw meat and tosses it to the cat.

"Consider the logistics," she says, turning back to me with a seductive smile. "I can keep you here as long as I like..."

The cheetah gulps down the meat.

"Why would you want to do that?"

She takes a moment, studying my face.

"Do you even know why you're here, Max?" she asks, taking a sip of mint tea.

"I came for adventure and to find some lost diamonds. But it was a lie and I'm stuck in Timbuktu."

"Perhaps it's time you heard the truth," she says, putting down the cup.

"What truth?"

"The truth about why you're here."

"I know why I'm here. I'm here to try to find the missing diamonds."

"What if I told you there are no missing diamonds?"

It gives me pause.

"Maurice told me..."

"Maurice lied," she interrupts. "Maurice works for me. You've been recruited."

"Recruited for what?"

"Take it as a complement. We're particular about whom we invite in."

"I have no idea what you're talking about..."

"You happen to fulfill our requirements. You're well connected, educated, a man of taste. You're American. We have potential business in America. You and your family have friends in high places. And we've made you into a killing machine. On top of all that, I like you. That much you know..."

She sits back, waiting for a reaction.

"Who are you? Is your name even Edwina?"

"I'm sure you know who I am," she says, ignoring the probe. "I owe my success to a policy of secrecy, illusion and deceit that protects my interests and guarantees my future. Lying to you was a necessity. You'll have to get used to how I operate."

"I could never get used to that. A criminal organization that owes its success to secrecy and deceit. Are you serious?"

"Silly boy, when you killed Sehrgitz your fate was sealed," she purrs, taking her time. "He was a man of influence. You're a fugitive. Lily is also a fugitive. But I'm offering you both a second chance. Who knows what awaits you out there in the big world? With me, you'll always be safe. You'll never want for anything. People will respect and fear you. You'll have power, dominion, and wealth beyond your wildest dreams."

"Why should I believe you? You lie about everything."

"If you don't believe, just look at the good fortune that comes to all our recruits."

"Where are they? I don't see them."

"You know the Banker. You've met Fasi. We have representatives in every major country except America."

"What do you want from me?"

"We want you to be our agent in the United States."

I'm taken aback.

"What? How does Maurice fit into all this?"

"Maurice is just a recruiter and an enforcer. Sometimes he can be reckless. He has an unfortunate tendency to think he can throw his weight around. Then I have to spank him."

"He tried to rape Lily. He needs more than a spanking. Don't you have a personal relationship with him?"

"Did he tell you that?"

"He suggested you might be more than friends."

"A thing of the past."

"So now he's turned his attentions toward Lily. But she's not interested. That makes him dangerous."

"Dangerous men like Maurice can be useful," she says. "You've shown you can be useful, too, Max. And quite dangerous, yourself."

"We're not going to play your game, Edwina, whatever it is. The whole thing's getting way out of hand."

She rises and begins to pace slowly.

"Max, let me give you some advice," she says, wringing her hands. "I want you to listen to me. Watch out for Lily. Don't let her get too close."

"What are you saying?"

"She's beautiful and you may think exotic. But don't let that girl fool you. She's a clever manipulator with devious designs. Don't believe anything she says."

"Why should I believe anything *you* say?"

"Because I have an investment in you. I want to protect that investment and I believe Lily has your ear. I believe she wants to use you to her own advantage."

"How so?"

"She thinks you're her ticket to freedom from slavery and a new life."

"I'm happy to give her freedom and a new life."

"You're so young, so naïve, poor boy. You can't see past the charade. Just a babe in the woods."

"Sadly, you're the one who can't see. Lily and I are in love. You wouldn't know love if it hit you in the face."

She chortles to herself, sits back down, and shakes her head.

"Have you ever even been in love, Max? You're too young to even understand the concept!"

Before I can answer, she says:

"Let me tell you about your precious Lily. I've treated her well...."

Now she's on her feet again, pacing.

"I've lavished gifts upon that miserable slave girl, given her my affection, treated her in every way like a princess. But she's not responded in kind. Instead of appreciating my generosity and hospitality, she's let me know that all this splendor I've given her is not enough, that she could somehow find a better life. Can you imagine? Such cold-heartedness, such ingratitude! And I believe she'll try to manipulate you to facilitate her wishes."

"Don't worry about me, Edwina. I can think for myself. My advice to you is, don't underestimate Lily," I say. "She's every bit as strong as you are. You'll never be able to tame her. So why bother? Why not just let her go?"

There's a pause as she continues pacing.

"You've no idea how lonely it can be out here in the colonies," she says after a few moments, as if talking to herself, or someone unseen.

Is this a new tack?

"We're outcasts in the wilderness... among wild beasts and savages..."

"Edwina? Isn't that the whole point?" I cut in. "Solitude and beauty. Isn't that what you want? Isn't that what most people eventually want?"

She seems to snap out of it.

"It can be surprisingly lonely in a place like this," she says, focusing her attention back on me. "Aside from that, everything you see, the world I've fashioned here, is mine and mine alone. It's my masterpiece. I've created a private paradise, Max. My castle in the desert. Nothing happens here without my blessing."

Her face is aglow with glee, as if she'd just had a eureka moment.

"What about El Gato? Where is he? I want to talk to him."

She returns to her seat.

"El Gato will never talk to you because *there is no El Gato*!" she says. "There never was!"

It takes a moment to sink in.

"El Gato... doesn't exist? The whole world terrified of him? No one speaks with him? What are you saying?"

"Only the myth of the notoriously elusive and mysterious El Gato is real," she says, back on her feet and pacing again. "I myself created the legend. Just the illusion keeps me safe, out of the spotlight, far from dangerous, prying eyes. I'm free to run my operation from Timbuktu without interference."

"You're El Gato?"

"You might say..."

"I'd say you're suffering delusions of grandeur, Edwina," my genuine concern showing in my voice. "And you're not well. Is all this elaborate drama and theatrics really necessary?"

She sits, settles back in her chair and takes the full measure of me.

I force myself not to be distracted by her seductive skills and remarkably youthful looks.

"We're talking about the art of illusion," she says, regaining her composure. "This is my world. Now it's your world. You belong to me now, Max. Get used to it."

"I don't belong to anybody. Nor does Lily."

My mind churns with wild thoughts.

How to negotiate with a madwoman?

"Look at your situation," she says casually, with a flip of her hand. "You're in Timbuktu and there's no going back. Forget about your old life. Like it or not, this is your future." Then, with emphasis: "Be grateful you even have one!"

It's clearly no use. I'm fighting a rising tide of panic, caught in a trap with almost no hope of making my way back to civilization.

But anger overrides fear.

"Haven't you been listening?" I demand to know, just short of a shout. "Lily and I want out. Our minds are made up."

Edwina pauses to take a sip of tea, never taking her eyes off me.

"Well, you see, Max, I have a serious problem," she says. "I've entrusted you with the keys to the kingdom. Now that you know my deepest secrets and how I operate, now that I've invited you behind the scenes and into my tent I can't let you go."

"Are you threatening me?"

"I'm merely describing your situation, trying to reason with you."

"It's no good, Edwina. This is a crazy house. Everything's smoke and mirrors. Lies are truths, truths are lies. How can anybody live this way? We need to go."

She makes a sweeping gesture.

"There's a hidden squad of armed men here. You know I can keep you both as long as I like."

Then she's on her feet again, starting to circle me.

"You have nothing to fear from us, Edwina. We won't give you or this place a second thought the minute we're out the door. Our own futures have nothing to do with you or this place. We can part as friends."

She begins pacing faster, orbiting me.

"You disappoint me, Max," she says, again wringing her hands. "Oh, how you disappoint me! I find this all very troubling, very troubling. Such ingrates, both of you!"

After a moment she comes to an abrupt halt directly in front of me.

"This is very irregular!" she declares.

Something in her voice makes the cheetah hiss and bare its fangs.

"I can see your muddled mind's made up," she snaps. "I can see in your case there's no hope. Perhaps you're not the man I thought you were! So I'll make an exception. Go ahead... see what happens!"

"Is that a threat?"

"Just understand what you're getting into. Once you're beyond the gates of Timbuktu you're on your own. This time there's no Maurice. He's definitely a bad boy but he's *my* bad boy."

I seize the moment.

"We'll need horses."

"I'll have horses saddled and ready by dawn. I'll even provide you with the means to protect yourselves, for whatever good it will do. The desert's dangerous. Frankly, the chances of surviving a journey into the Sahara by yourselves are slim to none. On top of all that, you're a wanted man, Max. And so is Lily. You're making a big mistake..."

When I say nothing, she adds, "It's not too late to reconsider, if you want to think about it."

"There's nothing to think about."

20

At dawn, four mounted riflemen escort us to the city gates. I'm armed with my service pistol, a Mauser infantry rifle, five gallons of spring water, three pounds of dry tack, a pound of coffee, serrated battle knife and enough ammunition to fight a small war. Lily's armed, as well, and has her own kit.

To the north, a thousand unbroken miles of some of the cruelest desert in the world. To the south, the darkest heart of uncharted Africa. Not a village or settlement within two hundred miles in any direction.

The guards salaam goodbyes so solemnly I doubt if they ever expect to see us again.

When the gates close behind us we're surrounded by a prevailing silence, facing the desert alone.

I look about, squinting against the glare and shimmering heat, scanning every direction, all the way to the horizon. It's a familiar scene. Not a sign of life. Not even a blade of grass. The hardships of desert life. Loneliness and despondency visit you in such a moment.

I mustn't let Lily see.

But she's smiling.

"It's beautiful, isn't it?" she says. "We're free."

She's right. It's beginning to feel almost like home.

We move on. After a while, I break the silence.

"I suspect they're not yet done with us. I think they intend to intercept us."

"Why do you say that?"

"Edwina's up to something. She's made it far too easy to escape."

"Edwina's crazy."

"She may be crazy, but we should never underestimate her."

"What do you think she'll do?"

"She knows we're too much of a threat and she'll come after us. She's a lioness in a woman's body, a real man eater, and she'll pleasure herself in the hunt until we capitulate or die trying to escape. My guess is she'll make a dangerous game of it, turn the whole thing into an exotic blood sport. And she'll probably bring backup with her. If I'm right, she wants to make us disappear, or force our return, and we're going to have our hands full to make sure that doesn't happen."

"Why would she come after us if she knows we're heavily armed? She armed us herself!"

"That's precisely my point. It's the ultimate sport. The ultimate thrill. She'll have the advantage and she knows it. We're going to have to surprise her."

"Perhaps you're right," Lily says. "But I'm not afraid."

When an oasis finally starts to take shape as a ripple on the horizon, the horses are beginning to falter, debilitated to exhaustion by the heat. When we enter the perimeter and continue towards the watering hole, I see potential danger in the eyes of every fellow traveler who glances my way.

As night falls, we make camp on the periphery near a corral. If there's anything strange, even the slightest disturbance in the surrounding darkness, the assembled horses in the small paddock will sound an alarm. By the time the fire flickers to glowing embers, the entire camp of Berbers and Tuaregs have settled in for the night, and all is quiet.

Lily sleeps tonight beyond the reach of firelight, out of sight in a small tent. But I must stand guard. So sleep never comes. I stay alert but calm, resting in a kind of wakeful slumber. The plan is to decamp at three a.m. and slip away further north.

I hear a startled whinny and hoof stomping sometime around two and come fully awake. In moments the noises stop, and the horses seem to return to normal. But I remain alert, crouching, knife in hand, motionless.

The silence is complete once again. I strain to hear. Not a sound.

Then, just as I prepare to relax, I sense danger, not specific but surely detectible somewhere nearby to my left, a presence just beyond whatever weak trace of visibility still lingers from the near-dead fire. I take a cautious step back, then another, tensely hovering, safely hidden in the night.

Now I see a dark shape inching forward, then moving swiftly and silently to the field blanket I've packed with my kit to make it look like someone was sleeping on the ground. His raised arm is gripping a knife. He glances in my direction and without hesitation comes at me, the knife still raised.

My quick sidestep dodges the downward strike and a simultaneous sharp forward thrust plunges my knife deep into the assassin's chest. I pull back and up with a ripping motion. He grunts and collapses gracefully and gently at my feet.

No man is alone in the desert.

Likely, there'll be more.

Keenly alert in the profound silence that follows, I listen and watch, waiting for a second attack.

But none comes.

Lily approaches in darkness.

"Who is that?" she whispers.

"I don't know. Maybe a horse thief. Or maybe a man sent by Edwina."

We bury the body a short distance away in the purplish gloam that precedes the desert dawn. Then we smother and hide any trace of fire, saddle up, and push on.

Less than an hour later, as dawn turns to day, we can make out five riders a half mile ahead. As they close the distance and draw near, it's clear they intend to block our way.

I focus my binoculars on the riders.

"I was right. It's Edwina. She has men with her. She means to stop us."

"What do we do?"

"I'll talk to them."

I unsheathe the Mauser, cradle it, and wait.

Edwina is flanked by Maurice and an armed guard. The other two riders are behind.

"Hello, Max," Edwina says.

"I knew you wouldn't stop toying with us. I knew you'd never let us go."

She regards us both with catlike interest and an intense, thin smile.

We're her prey.

"You never gave me a choice, so here I am. The odds are not good. Five against two. But even now, Max, it's not too late."

"Edwina..." My voice is strong, my words slow and emphatic. "You never intended to let us go. Sadly, you're not in your right mind. Maybe that's what this place does to you. It benefits you nothing to let us go. You said yourself you think we'll die trying to survive."

"Max, it's you who's crazy if you think you think you can just walk away from me and all I'm offering. If that's the game you want to play, you can't win. Do you know what an endgame is?"

I consider the odds. Five to two. They're all armed. Edwina and Maurice are veteran shooters.

"Winner takes all, you mean?"

"That's right. Your chances of survival are not good. But there's no need for violence. You're a beautiful boy with so much to look forward to. Please reconsider."

My calculus tells me that I can take out one, maybe two. Even three. The fourth or fifth would likely get me. Lily will have to even the odds.

"Lily!" Edwina calls out. "You don't belong here. Go home!"

"This is not my home!" Lily shouts back, malice and vengeance in her voice.

Lily mutters to me: "Max, I want Maurice."

I decide.

"You'll have to be quick, and you can't miss," I tell her. "Can you also handle one of the guards riding behind?"

"Yes. I won't miss."

"Then here's what we'll do."

I explain the plan.

"Let your horse protect you. Don't shoot unless they make the first move. No killing unless we have to. Maybe we can still just walk away, and they'll let us go. But be prepared. If they stop us it will happen fast."

"I am ready."

"All right. Look relaxed."

We cue the horses and move off at an easy pace in different flanking directions.

"Hold on there!" Edwina shouts. "Where do you think you're going?"

"Leave Lily out of this," I say. "She's just getting out of harm's way."

"Hold it right there, Max. I won't warn you again."

"You'll have to shoot me, Edwina. But what's the point? What good will that do?"

"Don't make me do this, Max."

"Your call, Edwina."

The rifle, resting now across the saddle and adjusted to rapid fire, is almost aligned at a square angle with the armed guard flanking Edwina. If I'm to get Edwina, I'll have to get him first. Lily, too, has moved into a broadside position, facing Maurice on the far side.

Lily opens up suddenly, without warning. She fires four rapid pistol shots, striking Maurice twice and knocking his horse out from under him, then hitting one of the backup guards who slumps and falls off his horse with a look of surprise on his face. Maurice and his horse go down together in a kind of violent slow-motion ballet just as Edwina, shooting from behind the flanking armed guard, gets off a shot that hits my horse. Then she wheels and tries to fire at Lily. As my horse goes down, I unload a thunderous rifle volley of several rounds blowing the guard off his horse as he tries, unsuccessfully, to aim his pistol at me. He falls into Edwina. She takes a shot from Lily that sends her flying backwards into the sand. The second backup rider fires at me once, then twice, hitting me with a wild shot that creases my abdomen just as I blow him off his horse with the Mauser. His horse bolts and runs away.

It's over in seconds.

I manage to stay on my feet as my horse goes down. As the smoke clears, I feel a warmth and realize I've been hit. There's no pain.

Lily's the only one still mounted on the only horse still standing.

There's movement on the ground. Lily dismounts, apparently unscathed, pistol in hand. Maurice, wounded and bloodied, suddenly rolls over and tries to aim a shot at Lily. But she steps up and shoots him in the chest, then again in the head.

The three armed guards are dead. But Edwina is still alive, struggling to grasp one of her pistols which has fallen to the ground just out of reach. I kick the pistol away and crouch down beside her. I tear a piece of her shirt to tie a tourniquet to her leg and pack her chest wound.

"You've ruined me...ruined me!" she hisses through her teeth, forcing the words. Her voice is weak, but her eyes blaze with fury.

Then, exhausted by the effort, she seems to deflate.

"Max," she says after a moment, her voice ebbing to no more than a whisper, "I gave you every opportunity... I could have made you somebody, given you riches beyond measure..."

I put my hand on her forehead.

"It was good while it lasted, Edwina. I'll always remember that special night," I tell her. "But you bet high and lost big. Now look where we are. I'll never understand what you were thinking."

She closes her eyes.

"I had power, riches, empire...I had it all...I should never have let you go..."

She's sinking.

"Why did you?"

She rallies her strength, fighting the darkness.

"For sport... sport! It's all a game...a beautiful game..."

"This is no game. This is shoot-to-kill. You know it."

"Nobody was supposed to die..."

"You wouldn't hesitate to kill us. You came here to kill us."

"I don't understand...how it all went wrong..."

"You underestimated both of us, Edwina. Maurice is dead. Your armed guards are dead. Horses are dead. You've been shot. I've been shot.

That's your endgame. Hope you enjoyed the show."

"Am I dying?"

I don't answer.

"Please help me..."

She winces against the pain.

Lily walks up with her pistol in her hand.

Edwina's glazed eyes turn to her.

"Help me, Lily..."

"You taught me to shoot first." There's seething vengeance in her voice.

Lily pulls the trigger.

"Lily!" I cry out, jumping to my feet. "You shot her!"

"It's better this way, Max. Alive she would chase us forever. And when she tires of that, she would kill us."

I scan the horizon. No sign of life. But I know it's only a matter of time before search parties set out to find Edwina. The entire organization could mobilize within days.

"You're bleeding..."

I glance down and pull up my shirt. There's a surprising amount of blood but the wound's no more than a graze.

"It's nothing..."

I stanch the bleeding with my linen neck scarf and look around. Any attempt to make an escape out of Africa across the Sahara under the best of circumstances is likely to fail. But with just one horse, it's bound to end tragically. Add an army of pursuers bent on vengeance, and ground travel is out of the question.

"We eliminated one threat," I tell her. "But we've got two more. Edwina's possible backup troops and the desert itself."

"So what do we do now?" Lily asks.

"Max?"

"Yes?"

"What do we do?"

"We fly."

21

"We can't just leave them here," Lily says, gesturing towards the bodies.

"There's no time."

She glances up. Vultures are already beginning to form in a tightening circle.

"Look," she says, pointing. "The vultures and night predators will do our work for us. Desert hyenas will come from many miles. By morning, everything, even the horses, will be gone. Even the bones."

"How do you know?" I ask.

"This is how mountain tribes in my country bury their dead. They call it the circle of life."

We strip the bodies, bag clothes and footwear, pistols, rifles, ammunition, water, trail food, cash, trinkets, pocket watches and identification. Maurice's Enfield Pattern 1914 sniper rifle has a telescopic sight and special suppressor adaptor to kill sound. This we carefully keep safe.

We load everything on Lily's horse and set out on foot across an uncharted stretch of wilderness in the direction of the aerodrome.

"How do we find the red bird?" she asks.

"With this," I say, showing her the compass. "We'll also follow the arc of the sun, and we know the horse will smell water before he can see it."

We arrive without incident near the end of day, pitch camp inside the oasis, make a fire, draw water from the spring.

"There are asps here," Lily says, as darkness descends. "I will show you something. Fetch me a tether."

"Tether?"

"Do you have rope?"

I pull a coiled length of oiled trail rope from a saddle bag. Lily takes the rope and disappears into the darkness. A moment later, she returns and arranges the rope in a circle around the campfire area.

"What are you doing?"

"No snake will pass," she tells me.

"A piece of rope will stop a snake?"

"A piece of rope soaked in human urine will stop any snake. It's tribal custom. They say that the urine of the most delicate woman is more offensive to a snake than the urine of the most virile man."

"You pissed on my rope?"

"Yes. Of course. That is why I went into the darkness, so you could not see. Would you rather sleep with the snakes?"

Remembering Maurice's dispatch of the asp cozying up in my crotch, I immediately express my gratitude.

Later, in the flickering light of a dying fire, she slips under the field blanket and coils her body against mine. The lovemaking is feral, violent, nothing like the little poke under the apple tree back home. I crush her in my arms as we roll and thrust together in a tight knot, two wild beasts in the throes of a hot and passionate battle rising as one into an explosive, spasmatic climax that leaves me drenched in sweat, my mind spinning, lying flat on my back, gasping for air.

Sometime later in the deep of the night I open my eyes to find Lily wide awake, lying next to me, studying the stars.

"What are you thinking?" I ask.

"I'm thinking about us."

She gets up on an elbow and looks at me.

"What are *you* thinking?"

"I'm thinking it's been the strangest day of my life. We killed five people today. We knew three of them. How do you feel about that?"

"I feel good."

"No sadness or remorse?"

"Sadness or remorse? In Africa, you don't have time for sadness or remorse. Otherwise you wouldn't have time for anything else,"

After a moment she adds:

"But I do have one regret..."

"What do you regret?"

"I've never told anyone. I'm so ashamed..."

She seems reluctant to continue.

"You can tell me, Lily..."

"I don't even know how to read..."

I draw her down and cradle her in my arms.

"My darling, where you come from no girls get an education. But you're very smart to have learned to speak English and French just from hearing it. "You'll get your education," I tell her. "You needn't worry..."

"No, Max. It's more than that. I want to read lots of books. I want to learn about the world. I want to travel. I want to know everything. That's my dream."

"You can have it all, Lily. I promise."

"I don't want to rely on anyone, Max. I want to be an educated woman. I want to have knowledge. The way you do. Then I can have power and rely only on myself. But first I need money. Just like a man."

"You don't have to think about money, Lily. I can provide whatever you need, including an education."

"You still don't understand, Max," she says. "I appreciate what you want to do. But I don't want your help. I don't want anybody's help. I want to do this for myself."

I feel as if she's slipping away.

"We can do this together, Lily," I tell her. "We can have a home. We can have a family. You can have anything you desire. I want to spend the rest of my life with you."

She puts her hand on my face.

"Thank you, Max. I feel the same. We can have all this. But first I have my own plan."

"What's your plan?"

"I'll let you know when the time comes. It's for both of us."

"Both of us? Now you've got me thinking..."

She rolls over on top of me.

"Stop thinking so much, Max," she says. "Do it again."

22

A few hours later we're approaching the gate of the nearby aerodrome, where two legionnaires, one tall, the other short, welcome us back and wave us in.

"How are the flying lessons going?" the tall one asks in French.

"I have a good teacher," Lily says.

"She's a talented student," I say. "She'll be flying solo soon."

"How's the fuel?" I ask.

"Always full," the short one says.

"Good. We'll need it. We'll be doing cross country today, practicing navigation and terrain landings. Don't expect us back until late."

"Yes, sir," the tall one says.

Two other legionnaires are already pushing the Spad out to the end of the dirt runway.

"Where do we fly?" Lily asks.

"There's a drought, so we'll track north and east away from the desert toward the Niger River.

The animals seeking water will navigate. We'll follow the river north. There's another airfield I heard of, and if the scavengers and vultures did their job back there, we'll have no pursuers."

We stow the bags and gear in the Spad's cargo bay and climb aboard.

A legionnaire cranks the propellor. The Spad comes alive with a throaty rumble and trembles like a racehorse eager to spring out of the gate. When the brakes release, she plunges down the runway and roars into the sky.

At five hundred feet we swing low to get a better look at a herd of desert elephants following an ancient game path to the river. Further on, we soar over giraffes, gazelles, antelopes, and a mob of ostriches sprinting almost as fast as we can fly. A small pride of desert lions shadows the antelopes.

By the time we finally reach our destination it's late afternoon and we've burned most of our fuel.

"Can you see the airfield?" I shout over the roar of the engine as the Niger looms into view on the far horizon.

"I see only river."

"Look for color. That will be a windsock. You can see it for miles."

"I see it."

It's another two minutes before I finally spot the tiny orange speck in the infinite wilderness below.

"You have the eyes of an eagle!" I shout back.

"I am an eagle!"

We make a slow, low pass over the aerodrome to chase off animals grazing on scrub grass, then make our approach in the last of the light. We roll to a stop and the roar of the engine finally quits, replaced immediately by an immense silence that swallows us whole. We marvel at the sudden peace and quiet. Stars are already bold as diamonds in the vast dome of endless night sky.

We're preparing to make camp when a figure emerges out of the darkness. As he raises the lantern, I can see he's wearing a ragged German infantry uniform.

"You speak English?" he asks in a heavy German accent.

"We need gasoline," I answer.

"Petrol is expensive."

"How much do you have?"

"How much do you need?"

"Enough to fill our tanks."

"You will need a lot of money for that."

"How much is a lot?"

"Two hundred fifty US."

I turn to Lily. She's stiff and pale.

"What's wrong?"

She doesn't answer. I'm not sure she's heard me.

I turn back to the German.

"I could buy the whole plane for less than that. We'll give you twenty dollars cash."

"You joke. You are in no position to negotiate. Petrol is scarce. What else do you have?"

"Clothing, war surplus. You could use a new shirt. New pair of pants?"

I pull a canvas duffel from the cargo bay.

"Forget your fucking clothes. What about her?" the German says, eyeing Lily. "I'll trade petrol for your whore."

"She's not for sale or trade. And she's no whore. She's my wife."

"You don't have a choice."

A second man steps from the darkness pointing a Luger at me.

Two rogue mercenaries.

Bandits.

"I'll have to speak with her," I counter.

I turn to Lily. She doesn't move.

Her eyes are dark.

She seems to be in a trance.

"I know this first man," she says calmly. Her voice, almost unrecognizable, gives me chills.

"You know him?"

"I know what to do."

"Lily?"

"Don't worry. I know how to handle this."

She turns slowly toward the bandits, seemingly relaxed, a coy smile on her face.

There's a long moment as the Germans begin to respond, practically drooling, unable to believe this welcome but unexpected stroke of good luck.

Still smiling seductively, Lily takes two long strides in their direction, then whips out a pistol and fires repeatedly.

The bandits, their faces flash-frozen in shock, sink to their knees side by side, clutching their guts.

"You didn't kill them!" I cry out. "You had a straight shot and didn't kill them!"

She doesn't answer.

She's in an altered state.

"You filthy fucking whore," the German growls.

"Help...help me..." the other whines.

She strolls over to the first German, who's dripping sweat and struggling to remain vertical.

Elegant as a statue, she opens her jalaba to expose her breasts.

She's out of herself.

"Oh Jesus, Lily...Don't!" I shout.

Oblivious to me, she boldly taunts the German:

"Is this what you want? Take a good look. Because I'm the last woman you'll ever see."

"Fucking whore!" he snarls, his voice quivering in hopeless rage dripping with contempt. "You can go fuck yourself...!"

Quickly, she grasps his belt and jams the barrel of her pistol deep into his crotch.

Bending low, she hisses: "Look... into... my... eyes!"

The blast brings a roar from the German as his body jerks and stiffens. Sputtering, choking on his own blood, he collapses, dying.

A groan from the other German draws Lily's attention.

She's still in a trance-like state.

"I haven't forgotten you," she says. "You asked for my help?"

She presses the barrel to his forehead and pulls the trigger.

In the ringing aftermath of the blast, time seems to slow.

There's only the smell of cordite.

A vast silence sets in so completely it consumes the entire desert.

Then, to my surprise Lily suddenly bursts into tears, unleashing a primal howl that splits the night like the desperate cry of a wounded animal. Hearing me repeatedly call her name, she slowly turns, eyes wide, her face now distorted into a mask of sorrow and pain.

She drops the gun.

Stunned and confused, I rush to wrap her in my arms.

Her body convulses in sobs.

I hold her in my embrace until the sobbing subsides and breathing starts to come more naturally.

Still clinging to me, she mutters: "The first one...The one with the lantern...I recognized him...But he didn't recognize me...There were many Germans...Bad men... Mercenaries...He was the leader... He did horrible things to me...I never wanted you to know..."

She's shaking, struggling with the memory.

"I'm so sorry," I tell her, tightening my grip, trying to soothe her, make her feel safe. "It's okay..."

After a moment, she continues.

"I never thought I'd see him again," she says, still having trouble with her words, trying to keep it together. "My father did not sell me. The German mercenaries came to our house and killed him. That man raped and violated me in front of my mother and sisters. I was terrified. I screamed and screamed, and he beat me until I thought I was going to die. They degraded and humiliated us for three days and left us for dead. But that man took me as his slave and dragged me away. Then he sold me to the tribal king. Now you know..."

I rock her in my arms, horrified.

"It's okay now."

"How can you love me when you know such terrible things?"

I pull away and gaze into the timeless face of Nefertiti.

Her eyes overflow with tears.

"Oh, Max," she sobs, shaking her head.

Something achingly beautiful wells up inside.

I draw her back into my arms.

"I love you, Lily," I tell her gently. "That's all I know. That's all you need to know."

23

A gap under a nearby ledge leads to a cave. I drop pebbles into the open space and count the seconds until they hit bottom. Then I shove the bandits into the hole and wait until I hear the satisfying sound of faint thuds far below.

That night we don't light a fire for fear of drawing attention.

As we sit close together in the dark, Lily says, "Max, I have to tell you something."

"Is something wrong?"

"No. I have to tell you about Maurice."

She s wraps the field blanket around her shoulders.

"Do you remember when I said Maurice wanted me to run away with him?"

"Yes."

"It was more than that. He was going to betray you. He was going to betray everybody."

"What are you talking about?"

"Do you know the man they call the Banker?"

"What about him?"

"Maurice told me was planning to steal a fortune from the Banker. And he wanted me to help him."

"How could you help him?"

"He didn't explain. But he said he knew things about the Banker and was planning to blackmail him. I think I was supposed to be part of the plan."

"What did you tell him?"

"I told him I wouldn't help him. I told him to leave me alone."

"Did he leave you alone?"

"No. When I refused, he slapped me. He said if I ever said a word about his plot to overthrow the Banker, he would kill me. Maurice was the kind of man who would kill you anyway if he had no further use for you. Especially if money was involved."

"Why are you telling me now?"

"Because maybe he was right. Maybe the Banker deserved to be blackmailed. He said he knew the Banker was corrupt. The Banker was stealing."

"Did you believe him?"

"He said one night the Banker got drunk and confessed everything. He told Maurice he was looking for an accomplice. He said together they could overthrow El Gato. But Maurice turned him down."

"Why would he turn him down?"

"He said the Banker's drunk talk wasn't believable. He didn't become a believer until he pretended to reconsider. That's when the Banker, in an act of good faith, revealed a secret vault full of contraband diamonds he'd been siphoning for years. It was enough to fill a wagon."

"If all this is true, how did the Banker go so long without being detected? Why wasn't he ever caught?"

"Because he said he had El Gato's complete trust. It was the Banker, and the Banker alone, who kept the books and policed the diamonds, the cash, the business, everything."

"That's bad business. It invites all kinds of trouble. I can't believe Edwina would be so careless. Did the Banker even know Edwina was the real El Gato?"

"I don't know."

"Do you believe his story?"

"I think Maurice believed it."

"Well, that's not going to help us now. What do you think we should do?"

"You're asking *me*?"

"Lily, we've got few options. I came here to find the lost diamonds. There are no lost diamonds. I know what I think we should do. I just want to know what you think."

Lily gets up and walks toward the rising sun. She looks at it for a moment, then turns around and says:

"I think maybe we ought to pay the Banker a visit. We've got nothing to lose. And maybe something to gain."

In the distance, morning smoke rises from a village.

"I like how you think. Now I'll see if we can get gas, or at least food and a horse," I tell her. "Are you all right here alone?"

"I can take care of myself."

In the village, Berbers and Tuaregs haggle over camels. I find a French-speaking tribal elder with a white beard.

"I want to trade for a horse," I tell him. He directs me to a nearby enclosure where a Berber is watching over three Arabs, two mares and a stallion. For a small fee, the old man will come along as my representative to facilitate the transaction.

"How much?"

"Twenty dollars American."

"That's a lot. I will pay you ten if the deal goes through. If not, I will pay you nothing."

The old man protests. But when he sees I'm prepared to walk, he agrees.

The stallion, it turns out, is not for sale or barter.

"May I look at the mares?"

The mares, three and four years old, seem healthy and strong. The horse trader wants to know what I have to trade for one of them. I produce a watch, a ballpoint pen, and a pair of desert boots salvaged from our recent skirmish on the road from Timbuktu.

The trader, indignant and clearly viewing my first offer as inadequate --with the exception of the watch--makes a show of mock outrage and grumbles something to the old man.

I dig into the bag and pull out a man's denim shirt and linen trousers I had recently offered, unsuccessfully, to the dead bandits. I'm not surprised to discover that this offer, too, is unsatisfactory. The trader makes sure I understand the whole proffered package is beneath his dignity.

It's not until I produce a pistol that once belonged to Maurice that his eyes light up with keen interest.

He says something excitedly to the old man.

"Do you have bullets?" the old man asks.

"Yes. I have one box of shells. Twenty-five in a box."

The two men huddle briefly.

I place the bartered goods on a table. When the trader is satisfied, he hands over the mare.

"I will need a saddle."

"Saddle is extra."

In the end, I pay another fifteen US dollars for saddle and tack.

"Now I need food," I tell the old man. "Where is the market?"

The old man points over his shoulder and I bid him farewell.

By the time I make my way back to the aerodrome, Lily's taking shelter from the sun under a wing of the Spad.

"That is a nice horse," she says.

"Are you hungry?"

"I am very hungry."

I sit with her beneath the wing and hand her a round loaf of still-warm, fresh-baked khobz bread stuffed with a grilled goat meat spiced with a redolent mixture of cumin, cinnamon, cloves, ginger and mint. I watch her eat in silence, eyes closed, making contented sounds like a cat. We share a bottle of fresh goat's milk and a chunk of goat cheese.

"What would these people do without goats?" I ask.

"It is the same with my people," Lily says, pausing to speak. "Everybody has goats. Nobody has an aeroplane. It would be a shame to lose this big red bird. What are we going to do?"

"There's not much we can do. We can't fly it and we can't hide it."

"They'll know we were here," Lily says.

"Maybe not. I met an Englishman just now in the village. He saw us fly in. He came up to me and offered to buy the plane. He wants to ship it back to England."

"He must have a lot of money. Did he offer a good price?"

"A thousand US. I took it."

"That's a very good price!"

"He's coming to see the plane."

"I know. I can see him now," she says, pointing.

When I turn, I recognize the man wearing a pith helmet, safari jacket and laced hunting boots as he approaches on horseback.

"I won't give him our real names."

"Greetings!" the man calls out as he draws near.

"Allow me to re-introduce myself," he says, dismounting and touching the brim of his pith helmet. "My name is Cedric Hadran-Gould. You're American. Very unusual in these parts. We met in the village."

"Yes, I know," I say, coming out from under the wing. I reach up and shake his hand. "I'm John Wicks." I gesture toward Lily, who's emerging into the sunlight "This is my wife, Naomi."

"Pleasure," he says, tipping his hat.

He directs his gaze to the Spad.

"This is a lovely machine you have here," he says. "I've never seen anything like it. Why on earth would you want to part with it?"

"It's a long story. But where we're going, there are no planes, and you can't fly in."

"Must be an interesting place. Where are you going, if I might ask?"

"Where I come from, strangers don't ask. But we've got nothing to hide. We're headed to the mountains."

"I will ask no more questions," he says. "But it sounds like you're on an adventure. So am I. However, I'm at a crossroads. Don't know where to turn next. Are you going into the Atlas?"

"We are."

"As it happens, I have an eccentric uncle who disappeared into the Atlas a while back," he says. "Nobody knows where he went, or why, or even if he's still alive. Jolly old chap, if a bit odd, by the name of Sir Basil Wesley-Rhodes, Marquis of Salisbury."

Lily and I exchange glances.

"Name ring a bell?" the Briton asks.

"Interesting name," I say. "Would you like to have a closer look at the plane?"

"I would indeed," the man says. He secures the horse to a wire wing stay and slowly begins to walk around the Spad.

"Do you fly, Cedric?"

"I plan to. When I eventually get back to Britain. For the moment, I'm simply collecting."

"Collecting aeroplanes?"

"I only have two at the moment. Both war surplus. One of them, a captured Fokker, was given me by a base commander in Chad."

"Chad seems like an unlikely choice for a man like yourself," I tell him. "I would think Kenya or Tanganyika would be more to your liking."

"How so?"

"You look like a hunter. I see you carry two sheathed rifles and keep a holstered pistol at your side."

"As it happens, I am a hunter, of sorts," he chuckles. "Takes me all over Africa. I specialize in what the natives call devil beasts. Rogue elephants, lions, renegade leopards, and hyenas that have acquired a taste for human flesh. Once they've had human, they never go back. These animals roam far afield from their unusual hunting grounds, sometimes hundreds of miles, looking for human prey. They typically target a village. I was called into Chad for just that reason. A huge leopard. She stalked people day and night. I put out goats as bait. But she ignored them."

"Did you finally get her?"

"I did. Tracked her one night to an acacia tree, on a high branch eating a fresh kill, a young girl from the village who had been fetching water. Beautiful beast, that leopard. Regret I had to kill her. Bloody shame I couldn't have saved the girl. I shot the leopard and they both fell out of the tree."

"What brings you here?"

"Curiosity, I suppose. Having a look around parts of Africa I've never seen before."

"You say you're at a crossroads?"

"I'm thinking seriously about going back to England. Been gone since before the War."

"You have family?"

"I had a wife. No children. Thinking about starting over again. Just not sure there's a place for me there. That's why I'm buying aeroplanes. The plan is to start a private air service, deliver mail and fly people around England and over to the Continent."

"How will you get this Spad to England?"

"Can't fly it, and no airfields or petrol between here and the Med. I'll dismantle it, then crate the parts, then reassemble it when it gets to England. I wired a fellow who's flying in today from Nairobi to make arrangements."

"You must have pull in these parts."

"The only pull I have is money. That's the only pull anyone has in Africa. Speaking of which, here's your payment in full," he says, reaching into his jacket and handing me an envelope.

I open it and count one thousand dollars US.

"Since I'm expecting my agent this afternoon," he says, getting back on his horse. "Perhaps I'll see you and your wife here again. If not, safe travels. Enjoy your adventure."

"Thanks," I say, shaking his hand. "Where are you headed after this?"

"You've got me thinking about the mountains. It's certainly the right direction and It could be the start of my journey home."

When he's out of earshot, Lily says:

"Do you think he's telling the truth?"

"Why wouldn't he be telling the truth? He doesn't even know us."

"Can you be sure? It could be a trap. Maybe he knows who we are. Maybe he was sent to track us. Maybe we're the devil beasts."

"If he meant us harm, I think we'd know by now, Lily."

"You're too trusting. Maybe there's more to this than we know. Don't you think it's a strange coincidence about the uncle? Why is he a hunter in Africa if he is a rich man? Is somebody paying him lots of money to find us?"

"Judging from his refined accent, I'd say he's a British aristocrat. If the Banker really is his uncle, and his uncle really is a Marquis, he would have been born into money."

Lily gives it some thought.

"Maybe he wants us to lead him to the Banker. Or maybe he wants to lead us."

"Don't overthink it, Lily."

She gives me a side look.

"Maybe we can use this Englishman," she says.

"How?"

"Ask him to join us. Or he may suggest it. Let's say it's not a coincidence he found us. And let's say his uncle really is the Banker. And let's say he doesn't know we suspect anything. Then we can manipulate him. We can turn the situation to our advantage."

"I think you're being paranoid."

"Paranoid? What is that?"

"That means you have an irrational fear that everybody's plotting against you. Let's not worry about the Englishman. He's a professional hunter and tracker. If he wants to find us, he will. We have five hard days ahead and we need to keep moving."

24

By nightfall, we've logged another twenty miles.
At dusk, I shoot a juvenile bush hog and roast it
over the fire. We eat some and smoke the rest.
Waterbags are still almost full, so we end the day
hydrated and well fed. There's enough dry grass
for the horses. Lily pees on the rope and we lie
close to the fire. Sometime before midnight,
counting shooting stars, we drift off into a deep
and uninterrupted sleep, not waking until first
light, our strength restored. We'll need it. The next
few days will test our capacity to endure serious
hardship.

It's full summer now in north Africa.
Temperatures average thirty degrees hotter by day
than the last time I passed this way.

The next four days blur into a sickly haze of
savage heat and misery. On a particularly hellish
fifty-mile stretch of lifeless desert Maurice had
called the Frying Pan we encounter temperatures
hot enough to cook eggs on a rock. It's only when
we shiver against the cold in the freezing nights
that we find relief from the blast furnace of the
Saharan sun. After just three days we're rationing
what's left of our water. On the fourth day it's a
grim race to the finish, a final push to a remote

oasis I remember that lies off the camel trail in the southern foothills of the Atlas Massif.

On the fifth day my knees begin to buckle. Lily, never taking her eyes off the ground, struggles to put one foot in front of the other. Exhausted, depleted, down to our last drops of water, nearly delirious and close to abandoning all hope. I nearly weep for joy at the sight of snow-topped peaks looming ahead. As we draw closer, the horses detect the scent of water and break away, bolting off in a cloud of dust.

"Now we'll surely die," Lily says.

"Don't worry," I tell her. "We're all going to the same place."

Two hours later we mercifully drag ourselves into the oasis and collapse, fully clothed, into a pool of cool water that flows up from the earth. The horses graze nearby on lush grass fed by the spring.

"I smell balsam and fir," Lily says as we curl up together, exhausted, under a roof of palm fronds. "The last time I smelled balsam and fir I was six years old in Afghanistan."

We rest, sleep, eat and drink in a protecting grove of Egyptian date palms, free from the desert's deadly indifference, savoring the sweet air and cooler temperatures.

Lily sits cross-legged, saying nothing. I lie next to her.

"Two more days and we'll be at the Citadel," I tell her, breaking the silence.

"I love the mountains," she says, thoughtfully gazing up at the panorama of peaks. "But first we get the diamonds. Then we can talk about love."

"Is that your plan?"

"My plan is, if we find the banker I'm going to seduce him. That's how we're going to get the diamonds."

I pull myself into a sitting position and look straight into her eyes.

Her gaze is steady, unflinching.

"Lily...?"

"There's no love involved. It's easy," she says. "I will get everything I want and then it will be ours."

"That's too high a price to pay," I tell her. "It would kill me."

She looks away.

"This is my plan, Max. It's the best way."

"It's a bad plan, lily."

"No more killing. Nobody even gets hurt. Everybody will be happy. You'll see."

She's about to go on, but two mounted figures come into view, one on horseback, the other on a camel.

I look through the binoculars.

"It's the hunter. He has a Berber with him."

"I'm not surprised," she says. "You think this is just a coincidence?"

"Everybody comes this way," I tell her. "It's the only passage through the mountains."

The two men ride up. The Englishman tips his pith helmet.

"So you've decided to go home to England?" I ask.

"You helped me make that decision."

"Who's your friend?"

"This is Ahmed. I hired him to get me across the pan. I'd never attempt it alone."

"We could have used somebody like Ahmed. It damn near killed us."

"Might have killed me, too. But Ahmed's life is in the desert. We travel only at night. The camel carries three hundred liters of water."

He pauses to look around.

"Mind if we bivouac here for the night?"

Lily gives me a pointed look.

"My wife is indisposed. She prefers privacy," I answer. "You'll be more comfortable on the grassy pitch just to the far side of the spring."

"As you wish," the Englishman says, nodding amiably.

The Berber mutters a few words in Arabic.

"Ahmed has just informed me that he's returning to his tribe without delay."

The guide acknowledges us with a nod, gives a small salaam, turns his camel, and heads back out towards the open desert.

"It's been a hard trip. I could use some rest," the Englishman says. "I think I'll make camp and turn in. Perhaps see you tomorrow?"

When he's gone, Lily says, "I don't trust that man. Why would he want to camp right with us? Why is he tracking us? We need to have a talk with him."

In the morning, the camp is empty.

"He slept over there," Lily says, pointing to trodden grass. "Where do you think he went?"

"The only place he can go from here is there," I say, pointing to the mountains. "Behind us, only desert."

"He's on his way to the Citadel," Lily says.

"What makes you so sure?"

"Because that's where the money is."

25

The massif looms large for the next two days as we gradually wend our way to higher ground through rugged foothills.

"We ride all day, but the mountain doesn't seem closer," Lily complains as we pause for a rest.

"Distances are deceiving," I tell her. "My father came to Africa years ago. Mount Kilimanjaro was a hundred miles away. But it looked to be only twenty. The distance from the bottom of the north slope to the bottom of the south slope was ninety miles. That's the distance from New York to Philadelphia. It looked to be right there in front of him, stretching across the entire horizon. But the base of the mountain was actually five days' ride."

It's another full day before we arrive at the familiar plateau wedged into the gorge that overlooks the long valley we've just left behind.

"Why are we stopping?" Lily wants to know.

"Because this is the Citadel."

"But there's nothing here," She says, glancing around.

I point up.

"Look!"

An armed guard peers down from a high ledge.

"Listen..."

There's a low rumbling.

"Now watch..."

The great granite slab rumbles and begins to move, opening slowly to reveal a cavernous entrance.

Lily watches with growing trepidation.

"Maybe it's a trap."

"It'll be OK. We need to stick to the plan," I tell her. "There's nowhere to run and no place to hide. After this, it's bandits all the way to Marrakesh. If it's a trap, there's nothing we can do now. Just be mindful and ready for anything."

The giant maw yawns wide as a rail tunnel, revealing only shadow and darkness.

"You expect me to go in there?" Lily asks.

"I've been in there."

As I lead my horse through the gaping threshold, I turn to see Lily hesitate, then stop. It's only after a long pause that she reluctantly continues into the mountain and pulls up alongside.

"I have a bad feeling," she says.

"I understand. But you were right to suggest we come here. This is where the money is. And this is where we'll find the Banker."

"I think he's found us," she says, pointing ahead into the shadows.

Two armed Berber guards appear. We dismount and they lead the horses away. A door opens and a houseman appears, ushering us deeper into the mountain. Through another door we step into the well-lit great hall I remember so well from my last visit. The furniture's arranged precisely as I'd last seen it. At the far end a fire flutters in the monolithic fireplace. Before the fire sits a man reading a book in an oversized armchair.

"Strange thing about these mountains," says the Banker, as he sets aside his book and walks toward us. "Even in summer it can be quite nippy up here."

"You knew we were coming."

"I've been expecting you," he says. "Come in where we'll be comfortable."

We walk the length of the room.

"This must be the incomparable Lily," he says as we take our seats.

"You know about Lily?"

"I know all about Lily. Aiyana, isn't it? Quite a good shot, I'm told. Your reputation as a rare beauty precedes you. But you're even more beautiful than I had imagined."

"Thank you," Lily says modestly, blushing.

"How would you know so much about Lily?" I ask.

"I make it my business to be well informed. There's very little I don't know."

"I'm not surprised. You've an impressive library here."

"As a matter of fact, I'm just now reading a seminal piece I'm sure you're familiar with," he says. "'Dark History,' by Princeton Professor Charles Wentworth. An analysis of the failed human experiment. I believe you studied under Professor Wentworth?"

"I did."

"Are you familiar with this work?"

"I am... Is this just a coincidence?" I ask.

"Just a bit of research."

"Research on me?"

"You should be flattered."

"Why would you do such deep research on me?"

"Since you ask, Edwina had her eye on you. She wanted to enlist you. But I have other plans for you."

"What other plans?"

"It was time Edwina stepped aside. She's gone off the reservation, as Buffalo Bill used to say."

"But what about El Gato?..."

He makes a dismissive gesture.

"There's no El Gato."

"So you knew El Gato was actually Edwina?"

"I created El Gato. I created Edwina. Edwina works for me."

"She worked for *you*? I had it the other way around."

"Edwina's just a figurehead, my boy. Useful to be sure. And beautiful. Well-connected in the Arab world. But given to self-aggrandizement and delusional fantasies. I gave her wealth and dominion. But she's headstrong. Insatiably power-hungry and greedy. Been behaving badly lately. Very badly, in fact. Planning a coup, I fear."

"The more I think I know about this organization, the less I know," I say. "And the less I want to know, frankly. Reality, fantasy; Fantasy, reality; Truths, lies; Lies, truths. Everything's upside down and ass backward."

"Ah, but don't rush to judgment!" the Banker counters. "You must understand that in our business, blurring the lines between reality and fiction is a necessary precaution. And a large part of diamonds' mystique. If we do our job properly, there are always more questions than answers. Throws the wolves off the scent. Edwina understood that. She was once a newcomer herself."

"Why would such an unfathomable and slippery culture attract anyone?"

The Banker puts his fingertips together, as if in prayer.

"Greed," he says. "Greed, my boy. Beautiful greed. Everybody's got a price. What's your price, Max?"

"Money doesn't interest me. I've got money."

"Really? Then why are you here?"

"I came for diamonds."

"Well there you are! I'd call that greed. You can call it what you like. Either way, you've come to the right place. But what if I were to tell you that the greater part of that diamond treasure confiscated from the Confederate Army that I told you about is right here, not a hundred feet from where we sit? Enough diamonds to fill a king's bath."

Lily gasps out loud.

"You told us you were spending that diamond money restoring your family's fortunes."

"And so I did. But that was only a handful. The lion's share is still with me. It's the largest private concentration of pure cut diamonds in the world."

"What about the legendary diamond mines of Fucauma Fasi told us about?"

"All part of the fictional bait Edwina used to lure you and others to her. She'd heard about you from Maurice during the last days of the war. You fit her qualifications both at the operational level and at the more personal level. Ultimately, she was hoping to enlist you to overthrow me. But she was also a notorious predator of men. Collected them like some people collect cars or horses. Some disappeared. You're lucky to get out alive."

"The sheik we met in Marrakesh. Is he really a sheik?"

"Very much so, and the true son of Edwina. He knows she's always been a bit dotty. But if he catches wind of what's happened to his mother and knows that you've disappeared? Well, you can imagine he'll come after you with everything he's got. You may need some protection yourself. You may want to think about that."

"What about Fasi?"

"Fasi's everybody's favorite thief. But he's also an extremely dangerous man. For all his avuncular jocularity, he'd kill you soon as look at you. But he knows the business better than anybody. So we keep Fasi close."

"I thought he was an interesting man."

"He speaks well of you."

"Well, that's a relief."

The Banker grins broadly and leans back.

"I always say that working with Fasi in this business is like working with the devil. Or the Pope. Depending on the transaction."

"Sir Basil, are you trying to recruit me?"

"You'd make a fine catch, I'll say that. And you'd learn a great deal from Fasi. You'd see we've got quite a big playing field for you to exercise your skills and realize your potential."

I give it a moment to show my appreciation.

"I'm flattered. But not interested. More than diamonds, I really came for adventure. I honestly believed I was doing the right thing. But Maurice sold me a bill of goods and maneuvered me into murder..."

The Banker nods in acknowledgement and puts his cup down.

"To his credit, Maurice could always be relied upon to get things done," he says. "That was his singular talent. And I suspect he almost believed the story he was telling you. But none of that mattered to Edwina. She was simply counting on him to recruit you. Very few are ever targeted. And you should be pleased. But Maurice had become a cause for concern, as well. I recently made him an offer to test his loyalty. He fell straight into the trap. But then he simply disappeared. You wouldn't happen to know anything about that, would you?"

He gives me a pointed look.

There's a pause as Lily and I exchange a quick glance.

"Maurice is dead," Lily says after a moment.

"Yes, I know," the Banker says.

Another silence.

"You know about the ambush?" I ask.

"I have an eyewitness," he says and pushes a button.

A door opens. Cedric Hadran-Gould steps into the room and removes his safari hat.

"Join us," the Banker says. "I believe you all know one another?"

"Very clever, that business of leaving the bodies to scavengers," the hunter says. "Only an African would know about that. Must have been your wife's idea. But of course we all know she's not really your wife."

"So you've been tracking us all along," I say. "You did a good job of staying hidden."

"That's what hunters do. Bloody shame, though, about Edwina. Damned fine-looking woman. Lying out there naked, food for hyenas and vultures."

"I have no pity for her. She tried to kill us," Lily says flatly.

"I'm surprised she didn't," Cedric says. "Given she was a hunter herself, and a fine shot."

The Banker says: "It's a tragic end for a legend, but necessary. You saved me the trouble. The same for Maurice. Saved me the trouble there, too."

Cedric continues: "As for those other two wretches, commendable! No one will ever find them at the bottom of that deep shaft. Not even the hyenas."

I tell him: "You've been watching us every step of the way. Yet we never spotted you even once."

"In my line of work, stealth's the first rule of survival," he replies. "Not only helps bag prey but saves lives."

A male servant wearing a white jacket and white gloves appears.

"Would you care for a beverage?" the Banker asks.

"Do you have beer?"

"I'll have the same," Cedric adds.

"Anything else?" the Banker says, looking expectantly at Lily.

"Mint tea. Thank you."

"Max, what brings you back to the Citadel?" he says, turning to me.

"Diamonds!" Lily interrupts, energized.

The Banker turns back to Lily and gives her an assessing look.

"And what, pray, beautiful Lily, would you do with diamonds?" he asks, clearly charmed and genuinely curious.

"I would become rich!" Her smile is strikingly beautiful.

The Banker smiles indulgently, running his tongue over his lips, and gives her a long, appreciative look.

"How interesting...And what else?..."

"What else? I don't understand..."

"I know all about diamonds, Lily. I have lots of them. But nothing is free. There's a price for everything..."

"I have no money..."

"But you have other assets."

There's a heavy pause. My heart's pounding.

"I'd say that under normal circumstances this would be a private conversation," he continues, glancing briefly at me. "But let me be frank, Lily. You'd also be my friend. My *very good* friend. Do you understand what I'm saying?"

Lily does not turn away from the Banker.

The Banker glances again at me.

I say nothing. I don't want to hear this. I keep my eyes on Lily.

"I can become your friend," Lily answers without hesitation. She avoids eye contact with me.

"This would require, Lily, more than just a casual understanding," the Banker says. "It would require a commitment not just to me but to the organization itself. In other words, you would have to live here under my protection. What do you think of that?"

Lily stands, statuesque and regal, graceful and available.

"I think I'd like that."

My heart is breaking.

"Well, well," the Banker says, chuckling to himself. "Never underestimate the power of diamonds!"

He turns to me.

"Lily's not really your wife, is she?"

"She is not," I answer through my pain. "As you can see, she's her own person."

"You say, Max, you came back here for diamonds. But that's not really why you're here, is it?"

"I just want to get out of Africa."

"I'm sure that can be arranged," The Banker says matter-of-factly. "It happens my nephew's on his way home, as well. Cedric has provided valuable services for us over the years. But the business is changing, and Africa is changing. He can provide safe passage to Marrakesh."

I turn to the hunter.

"Is your story about collecting airplanes and starting an air service just another fabrication?" I ask.

"Not at all," the hunter answers. "In fact, your Spad is already in Mombasa as we speak. I'm looking for pilots. But I understand you're also a man of means. Might you be interested in entering into a partnership? I'm seeking a few private investors, people with an interest in aviation."

"I have other options back in the states, but we can talk about that," I answer. "I need to reconnect with my family. I haven't spoken to them in months."

"I quite understand," the hunter says. "We'll have plenty of time to talk on the way to Marrakesh."

"First, I need to speak to Lily privately."

26

When we're alone and the door to the guest chamber is closed, I confront Lily.

"I never thought you'd go through with it."

I can hear the hurt and bitterness in my voice.

Was Maurice right about her, after all?

"Why are you surprised? I told you I intended to seduce him. Does it matter that he thinks he's seducing me?"

"Doesn't it bother you that you'll be having sex and who knows what else with this complete stranger as often as he likes for as long as he likes?"

"No. Why should it?"

"How can you say that? What about us? You know how I feel about you."

She steps closer.

"He's a thief, Max. They're all thieves. You finally found your diamonds, and now you deserve your share. This is the only way we'll get them. It's our only chance."

"No, lily, not this way. I didn't think you'd actually give your body to the man."

"I feel nothing for him. I feel only for you. It's not about sex. It's about power. The one who has the diamonds has the power. Even as a girl in Mombasa I could see that! Just two diamonds could buy a house. One diamond could buy ten slaves."

She gently reaches to touch my face.

"It's the only way to get to the diamonds without ever having to fire a shot."

"I don't like it."

"I'm doing this for *us*, Max."

"And then what? What if the plan doesn't work? Do you have to kill the Banker? Is that how it ends?"

"You don't give me much credit. I'm not planning to kill anybody."

"Do you think the Banker's stupid? Do you think he's going to let you just walk in and take everything? He could have his way with you as long as he likes, and then just kill you."

"Do you think *I'm* stupid?"

"It's dangerous business, Lily. You'd have to be clever to pull it off. If you don't pull it off, it could end badly. If you do pull it off, it's a full-time job, a different life, and a very different world. It may take a long time and there's no going back. Think about that."

She moves even closer, a hint of sadness in her eyes.

"You make me happy, Max, happier than anyone has ever made me," she says, placing her hands on my shoulders. "You could teach me to love, and I could love you. But if you want the truth, right now love is not enough."

"Why not? To me it's everything. And you're everything."

She holds my gaze, looking deep into my eyes.

"I come from another world. Men used me and abused me. Why shouldn't I use them when I have my chance?"

"Was it all a lie with us, too?" I ask her, stepping back. "Have you just been using me?"

She drops her hands.

"No more than you've been using me."

"Using you! I'm not using you."

"Of course you are. We all use each other."

"Do you really believe that?"

"Yes, I do."

"I can't understand how you think."

"If you'd lived my life perhaps you'd understand."

"I don't think I'll ever be able to do that."

"Well then I'm sad," she says, turning away from me. "But this is the only answer for me. I must do this."

"Edwina warned me that this would happen."

"She wanted to turn you against me because she was jealous."

The full realization that everything's coming quickly undone begins to hit home.

"Lily, don't let yourself get sucked into this crazy idea," I beg, turning her to face me. "Can't you see? You were right all along. It *is* a trap. Even if you could somehow get to the diamonds he'd never let you go. You want freedom, but you're walking straight into slavery again! Don't you see that? Listen to me! There's still time. We're young. We can still have a life..."

"Max, if you love me and believe as I do that we have a future, please let me do what I must... until I have the power never again to be a victim. Until I have enough money to answer to no man..."

"If you seek wealth, how will you ever know when it's enough?"

She holds my gaze, then adds:

"This isn't about greed, Max... This is about us... Not until I first learn to love myself can I learn to love you."

Suddenly the words resonate. For the first time, I get a glimpse of what she's trying to tell me.

"I may not like what I'm about to do, but I know exactly how to do it. Someday, if you still want me, I'll be there."

I take her hands in mine and search her eyes.

"You're my life, Lily," I tell her. "I didn't ask for it. But that's how it is. If you ever learn to love, you'll know the pain I feel. My heart's bleeding. But I will get out of your way. I accept you have to do this for yourself. But know that in my heart, I can never let you go."

She steps forward and I wrap my arms around her.

"Thank you, Max," she whispers, returning my embrace. "Now I think I'm beginning to feel what you say you feel..."

I turn and walk quickly out the door, fighting the urge to look back.

27

As late as noon the following day, I'm still struggling to cope with two new unwelcome companions: loss and loneliness. The Hunter and I are another six miles deeper into the rugged high country that straddles the spine of the Atlas. I've kept to myself, not encouraging conversation, lost in a pall of sorrow, and surprised by how deeply I miss having Lily by my side.

"Thinking about your lady friend?" the hunter asks tentatively, after two hours of unbroken silence.

"She's on my mind," I tell him.

"Yes. I can imagine. Good looking woman. You must have a great deal to think about."

When I say nothing, he adds:

"Hope you don't mind my asking...what was she thinking? Afghani is she? Whatever she is, she's on dangerous ground. Playing with the devil himself. Basil's a notorious predator. She'll never see a penny, not a single diamond. And she'll be his slave for the rest of her days, until he decides to get rid of her."

Lily, I now know, is capable of almost anything and fears nothing.

"I wouldn't bet on it, Cecil," I say, giving him a side glance. "I don't think Sir Basil has any idea what he's dealing with."

He eyes me with a quizzical look.

"How's that?" he says.

I don't answer.

We ride on, higher and higher until we reach a small plateau. The vast empire of brilliant cobalt sky yields to mauve, then lilac. Finally, the sun's gone. Onrushing dark clouds greet us as we clear the crest.

"Storm coming. Better hole up here," the hunter says.

In minutes, howling wind and driving rain swoop in. We scramble for shelter under an overhang just as the first claps of thunder crash and lightning flashes all around.

Moments later, dry and protected from the downpour, we settle in and secure the horses. Curtains of rainwater splash over the outer edges of our makeshift shelter.

"Tuaregs in the area again," the hunter says, as he takes a mouthful from a large travel canteen in his pack.

"Finest American bourbon," he adds. "You might appreciate that."

He offers the big flask to me. The whiskey goes down smoky, hot, smooth, buttery and strong. Immensely satisfying to body and soul.

"The sheik's people killed so many bandits this year they're back with a vengeance," he continues. "All strangers are fair game. So we need to be invisible. We'll travel by night to avoid contact or capture. I understand you've had some experience with bandits?"

"Not Tuareg. Berbers," I tell him. "Maurice managed to get us out of that scrape without bloodshed. I was merely an observer."

"You're too modest. I know for a fact you've got notches in your belt."

"I never went looking for trouble."

"But when trouble came, you handled it."

"It was self-defense."

"Call it what you like. I need to know you've got my back. I gives me peace of mind knowing I don't have to babysit you if we run into trouble."

"I'd like to believe you can count on me. But I never fired a shot in the war. So far, I've been lucky. I don't want to push my luck."

"I'm hoping you won't have to," he says. "But we've got to be ready. The Tuaregs don't care if you've never fired a shot and only had a minor skirmish with Berbers. It's all the same to them. They're out for blood. While we can, let's enjoy the lull and maybe catch a little sleep. As soon as the storm passes, we'll move ahead."

After the rain and another hour of shelter, we press on into almost total darkness, letting the horses pick their way slowly down through the foothills of the Massif's north face.

By the time first light begins to creep into the rugged landscape, my eyes are heavy. I find myself nodding, then snapping back. But Cedric's undeterred, showing no signs of fatigue. In fact, he's keenly alert, riveted like a dog on the scent.

"Stop here," he says. "Take a look."

He hands me his binoculars.

"Perfect ambush country," I respond. "Lots of high ground."

"That's how I see it," he says. "But if they're out there they won't be expecting anybody this early. If they do show, they'll be on the hilltops and ridge lines. Conceal their horses in the arroyos and small canyons."

He looks up at the violet sky.

"Soon it'll be light enough to spot us. We need to hide. Let's wait and see. I'll keep watch. You might want to take a nap."

I stretch out behind a rock.

The next thing I know Cedric's jostling my shoulder.

"We have company," Cedric says. "They don't know we're here, but they're preparing a web for whatever fly may come this way. Whoever walks into the trap will get robbed or shot."

With my binoculars, I see figures taking positions along the ridges of both sides of the canyon ahead.

"I make out a dozen heavily armed men with rifles and bandeliers, six on either side."

Cedric stares intently into his binoculars.

"Looks like the sheik taught them a lesson," he says. "They're well prepared this time. Ready to attack, defend or plunder."

"Go 'round?" I ask. "What do you think?"

"It's a hike, but no other option," he concurs. "By nightfall, depending on terrain, we could be a day's ride closer to Marrakesh and out of bandit country."

28

Walking the horses, we make our way east, taking cover behind small hillocks, sun-blistered rock outcrops and patches of dense underbrush to mask our progress. Turning north, we blaze a path that snakes into knotted thorn scrub, up a steep rise, and through gnarled thickets. That leaves the bandits some distance to our west.

Or so we believe.

"Get down. Stay low," Cedric says, slipping off his horse. I dismount. Together, we ease the horses into a pocket of undergrowth.

"What did I miss?" I ask.

"Bandits along the rise to our left," he says. "They might have spotted us."

"I see nothing," I say.

"Took me years. By now second nature. Essential to my line of work," he says.

We wait in silence for five minutes, then take another look.

"Nothing now," he says. "But something feels wrong. Not a sign of anybody. Better check your pieces and ammunition. It could get warm if they come this way."

"If you don't mind being bait, I'll hide in the rocks above with a view of the field," I tell him. "I'll be able to see everything. I'll attach a sniping suppressor to kill sound if they come."

"Are you a good shot?"

"Count on it."

"I intend to."

"Could be just a false alarm."

"We'll know soon enough."

I attach the sniper's suppressor to Maurice's Enfield and move quickly up the rise to a vantage point that commands a dominant overview of the scene below. From here, I can observe the backside of the canyon where bandits had been preparing their ambush. With binoculars I can make out a camp with men and horses, relieved to see no sign of intruders in our vicinity-- until suddenly I notice movement nearby. Two masked figures in black turbans appear, cautiously peering over the top of a rock below. It's uncertain whether they can see the hunter. I spread myself prone on a ledge in ready position, tighten the stock sling firmly around my arm and shoulder, take aim through the crosshairs, and wait.

I can see the hunter, thirty yards distant, apparently unaware of their presence.

Could they have spotted him?

Has the hunter become the hunted?

Or are they just curious about a fellow traveler?

The answer comes quickly.

Both men produce Mausers, adjust the rifles into a firing position on the top of the rock, and begin to take aim.

For me, time slows. I breathe through my nose. Steadying my nerves, ignoring my racing heart, I focus my mind. Carefully, I place the head of the first assassin into the scope's crosshairs. Holding my breath, I tighten my grip, and slowly squeeze the trigger. Then the muted PHUT of the shot, the sharp kick of the .30 caliber round, and the bloom of scarlet where the top of the man's head had been. In less than a second, crosshairs on the head of the second assassin and another kick and another clean hit.

It happens so fast I realize I'm still holding my breath.

It takes a moment to come to the full realization of what I've done and adjust to a rush of conflicting emotions, the thrill and the horror, washing over me.

I'm about to make my way back down to the hunter when I notice a third, then a fourth, figure suddenly appear. They approach through a narrow gulch and take up positions not far from the hunter, who signals he's already aware of their presence. He moves swiftly to a new hiding place.

I drop low and press myself once again flat on the rock ledge. Through the scope, I navigate the crosshairs. Both targets wear black turbans and carry Mausers. They're unaware of their fallen comrades and have no idea I'm taking a bead from above. They move to a firing position. But when they discover their target's no longer there, they split up, rifles ready, stocks pressed to their shoulders. I shoot the first one, PHUT. He drops like a stone. At that instant the hunter appears from behind a rock and dispatches the second assassin with a knife.

I wait and watch, heart still racing, eyeing the landscape for signs of further hostile arrivals. The hunter ducks back into hiding. After several minutes, when it appears the field's finally clear, I join him.

The horses are ready to go.

"We need to put lots of miles behind us before they find these chaps," he says.

For the first mile, heading north, we walk briskly, leading the horses.

Back in the saddle, the hunter shouts:

"Bloody well done!" as we break into a steady canter. "Four down and not a sound!"

By the end of the day, we're twenty-five miles closer to Marrakesh.

After we set up camp with a small fire flickering against the desert night chill, Cedric, full of renewed enthusiasm, declares:

"That was a bit of damned fine work back there with those bandits. I Knew I could count on you."

I probe the flames with a stick.

"Something on your mind?" he asks.

"I've been thinking about what happened today. I appreciate what you're saying. But I'm not proud of what I've done."

He takes a nip from the whiskey flask.

"I wouldn't overthink it, old chap," he says. "It was them or us."

He hands the flask to me. I swallow the welcome heat, and hand it back.

There's a long pause while we both contemplate the fire.

"Pretty handy with that knife today," I tell him after a few minutes. "What did you do in the War? I don't think you've told me."

"British Expeditionary Forces, Africa, special ops."

"Special ops?"

"Night work, undercover, sabotage, sniper teams, close combat, that sort of thing. Learned a great deal from the Gurkhas. Do you know how Gurkhas penetrate an enemy's defense?"

He looks at me expectantly.

"No idea."

"They sneak up in the dark, quiet as the fog, and tickle a sentry's legs or ankles with a feather. When the unsuspecting guard looks down, they whack off his head with a bolo. Not a sound. Very effective."

"Did you have to kill a lot of people?"

"It was war."

"Does it ever bother you?" I ask.

"Never think about it. Why should I? What good would it do? Why should you?"

"I never killed anybody in the War. Never even fired a shot. But ever since, I seem to be leaving a trail of bodies everywhere I go."

He takes another nip, and so do I.

"Went the other way for me," he says. "Just wild game after the War --until today."

There's another pause.

"It takes a very special type of person to try to make a life in Africa," he says. "Most people either die trying or go home."

"I came to Africa on a lark," I say. "In search of diamonds. But diamonds turned out to be a terrible curse. Made me the kind of man I never wanted to be."

"How so?"

"What am I? I'm a murderer and a fugitive running for my life from an outlaw enterprise, looking to make a fresh start. And now I've lost the woman I love. All because of diamonds."

"If not diamonds, what is it you want?"

"It's not what I want that's the rub. It's what my father wants. He wants me to follow him into a job on Wall Street. That's why I'm here."

The hunter thinks about that for a moment.

"You can fly aeroplanes. There's a future in that."

"It's crossed my mind."

"Then maybe you should consider my offer."

"I'm thinking about it."

"Good. In the meantime, when we get to Marrakesh we need to keep a low profile, just in case the Sheik has discovered the truth of his mother's fate and has his people out looking for you."

29

Marrakesh slowly rises like an umber tsunami from the ancient dust of the desert. As we ride closer, we can see black tents and blue-robed Berbers herding belled goats over the sparse landscape on all sides. We pass an outbound camel caravan a quarter mile long and a man with a sad-looking dancing bear on a chain. When we enter the gates, we're both wearing burnooses and jalabas to hide our identities. To be safe, we split up and ride on separately, meeting at the home of an Arab friend of the hunter's, who gives us a meal of couscous, mint tea, and a place to sleep in the attic. Below us, visible through cracks in the floor, are the man's goats. The heat in the attic, stench from the animals, and voracious mosquitoes swarming in the thick air make for a miserable night.

We suffer through several mostly sleepless hours, then set out again in darkness for our final destination in Morocco.

By the time we finally get to Casablanca we've been in the bush three days dreaming about the welcoming refreshment and relief we might find at Fasi's. But when we arrive, his place is empty and

Fasi's disappeared. He's left no forwarding address and vanished without a trace.

"Something big must have come up," the hunter says, surveying the empty rooms. "Fasi's not the kind of chap to simply disappear. He's the kind of chap that makes other people disappear."

"Let me guess," I say. "You think it might have something to do with the disappearance of Edwina?"

"If so, there's only one reason he'd run."

"What's that?"

"The sheik. If the sheik's on to what's been happening and he's out to avenge his mother and his family honor, the first person he might suspect in a plot is Fasi. He might also go after the Banker. Fasi would understand that. He'd become invisible while he regrouped."

"If you're right, then there's a lot we don't know. I could also be a target."

"Quite so. I might suggest we lose no time getting out of Morocco."

Disguised in turbans and hooded jalabas, we make our way through a teeming market square packed with braying camels, snorting mules, shouting merchants and stray dogs. Then on we push through crowded, narrow streets to the port. There, in the stench of rotting fish debris, fishermen's flashing knives flay the wings from skates and toss their carcasses back into bloodied harbor water that boils with thousands of fish in a ferocious feeding frenzy. Swarms of screaming seagulls swoop down to scoop scraps off the seething surface. More gulls patrol the quay, slick with blood and fish guts, squawking and strutting and snatching up whatever doesn't end up in the water.

"Nature at work," the hunter says. "A wonder to behold."

He looks around. The cement, glistening with a slippery coat of fish scales that glitter like diamonds, is jammed with hundreds of fishmongers hawking fresh catch from carts and stalls.

"We seem to have blended in. Nothing out of the ordinary. Everything looks normal," he adds.

"How can you know?"

"More of an art than a science," he says. "A sixth sense you develop from years of reading the unreadable, things most people wouldn't even notice."

"Such as?"

"Such as a look or a glance or a blink of an eye, a shoelace, a cigarette, a shadow, any tiny clue, any hint of something out of the ordinary, no matter how small."

"You can see all that just glancing around?"

"A simple survival skill. Served me well as soldier, and hunter."

He pauses.

"And just now, as I'm speaking to you, I do notice something. Walk with me. Keep talking."

We set off again in the direction of the ships' pier where several large vessels are tied up.

"What do you see?" I ask.

"Two men. I believe they've been watching us. Could be common thieves, but I doubt it because we don't look like likely targets. Not in this disguise. Maybe it's something else. Keep moving."

"What should I be looking for?"

"White hooded burnooses. Moroccan. Khaki desert jackets. German surplus. They're together but one's wearing sunglasses, a bit unusual."

"Maybe we should split up."

"I'll meet you behind that roofed market up ahead where we can ditch this Arab wear," he says. "There's a ticket office there. We'll book passage on the Masara Queen. She sails for Marseilles tonight."

We make a show of goodbyes. I drift off to a nearby stall, pretending to examine trays of eels, drawing the cowl down further over my eyes. Out of the corner of one eye I spot the one with the sunglasses, then the other. They appear to be moving with urgency through the crowd. The one without sunglasses heads in my direction. The other continues on toward the docks. I leave the stall, but the first pursuer steps squarely in front of me, blocking my way. He demands I remove my cowl. I pretend to be hard of hearing, beckon him closer, motioning that I have something I want to tell him. When he steps in, I thrust up my clawed hand, seize his throat in a vice lock, and squeeze his larynx. Simultaneously, resisting a temptation to crush the larynx and finish him off, I pull him close with my other arm in a fierce embrace, muffling his frantic efforts to free himself. In seconds, the silent struggle ceases and he goes limp in my arms, unconscious.

But in my effort to spare a life, have I run an unacceptable risk? Will I regret I didn't kill him? I know from training with my Belgian Foreign Legion drillmaster I can expect the pursuer, whoever he is, to be out for an hour or so, and seriously disoriented after that.

No one seems to notice as I continue to hold him upright, patting him on the back like a long-lost friend. Moments later, I maneuver him to a nearby wall, where I gently position him in a seated position, as if he were taking a brief nap. Everyone nearby is so preoccupied with bartering, buying, and selling, they don't give the sleeping stranger a second thought.

Moments later, I duck into a small alley and shed the Arab disguise, leaving the jalaba folded neatly in an empty doorway.

When I find the hunter, he's quietly sipping a demitasse of thick Arabian coffee under a red and white umbrella in a small waterfront café. A mixture of expats, Europeans, and prosperous-looking Moroccan businessmen in suits and fezzes fill the seats. Cedric's comfortable and relaxed. He looks like a regular.

I join him and order a coffee.

"Where's your shadow?" I ask.

"I managed to get intel," the hunter says. "It turns out you're not a suspect, after all. The sheik smelled a plot and became suspicious of foul play when his mother went missing. He sent his best trackers to find out what's going on. My guess is the Banker and Fasi got word of his move and made themselves scarce. He just wanted answers and hoped maybe you could shed light on the mystery. That's the story he gave me. But I never trust a stalker. He could be lying to buy time until they can grab us. To be safe, I persuaded a gendarme to deliver him into the hands of the local French Foreign legion battalion, where I have a few friends. He'll be the guest of the Legion for a few days, until long after we're gone. Alive but harmless. And yours?"

"Incapacitated. Sleeping. He'll wake up. But he won't be a threat for the next hour."

"Still, finish your coffee, we'd better get on with it," the hunter says, putting down his cup. "I've booked passage. We can board the ship at any time."

30

When we finally arrive ten days later in the English Channel port of Dover in full military dress, we're greeted by a courtly-looking chauffeur in tailored livery who addresses the hunter as "Sir Cedric" and escorts us to a spanking-new Rolls Royce Silver Ghost that's half the length of a tennis court.

We pull through a private gate two hours later and proceed down a long, carefully groomed gravel drive several miles long that winds through woods and opens into a vast estate of rolling hills and meadows with herds of grazing sheep. It's crowned in the distance by a manor that looks to be the size of Versailles.

"I must say, it's good to be home," Sir Cedric says, taking it all in.

"That's some home," I tell him. "Does everybody call you Sir Cedric?"

"Here, yes."

"So, I assume you have a title?"

"Fifth Earl of Bletham."

"Earl? That's right up there with the top peers. Member of the royal family?"

"The King's my fourth cousin."

"I guess that puts you in line for the throne. And Sir Basil?"

"Second cousin to the King. But he's a pariah to the whole family because of the nature of his business. To some degree, so am I. But less so."

"If it's all the same to you, I'll just call you Cedric."

"Fine by me," he says, gazing out over the passing fields. "I'm delighted to see the sheep seem to be doing rather well. They've bounced back nicely. When the War began, the government requisitioned every last one to help feed the troops."

We roll on, getting closer to the great estate house.

"How big is this place?" I ask.

"Don't know," he says. "Never asked. But if you look around, everything you see, as far as you can see, is all Bletham."

"How long have you been gone?"

"It's been five years. After the War broke out we all thought we'd be home by Christmas. But then I found myself in Africa. When the War finally ended, things just seemed to happen. The next thing I knew I was hunting wild game."

I strain to take in the scenery on both sides.

"I don't see any aeroplanes."

"We've built an aerodrome on another part of the property some two miles distant," he informs me. "We'll go there in the morning, and you can decide if you want to be part of the coming revolution in aviation."

Ahead, we can see what looks like a small crowd.

"There'll be a bit of a fuss, now, but just act like it's all perfectly normal," he mutters.

An army of servants in full dress supervised by a butler in tails is lined up like a military parade at the entrance to attend the return of the master.

"Sir Cedric," purrs the butler, opening the car door. "Welcome home, sir."

The butler and I follow Cedric down the long line of a hundred or so housemen, footmen, house maids, chamber maids, cooks, gardeners, grooms, stable hands, carpenters, and assorted others, as Cedric pauses to accept a few welcoming words from each, until finally we're at a front door that dwarfs any front door I've ever seen outside a palace or a museum.

"Thank you all!" he shouts, turning to give a gallant wave to his flock in what looks like a practiced papal salute. We slide into the vast interior, accompanied by a few servants who disappear upstairs with the bags.

"Well, that's the worst of it," he says. "Now we can relax. Banes will show you to your room. You're on your own. I'm going to clean up and catch up on some correspondence. We'll meet in the dining room at eight."

Banes leads me up a sweeping curved staircase and down a corridor to my chambers, more of a grand old-world suite than a room. The staff has already put my things in dressers and drawers. Jackets are hanging in a closet. Fifteen-foot French windows are flung open to let in the abundant spring sunshine, with an accompanying breeze that smells like fresh-cut meadows.

At eight sharp Cecil arrives in a dining room dominated by a rectangular refectory table thirty feet long designed to accommodate sixty guests. But on this occasion, we take our meal, a multi-course extravaganza of meat, fish, and poultry, at one end so we can talk without shouting. Two liveried footmen in powdered wigs attend our every need, delivering courses and pouring wine. Cedric, long accustomed to this sort of thing, in spite of years of absence and hardship, looks right at home and takes it all in stride.

"The food's very good," I comment, just as he digs into a slab of rare roast beef thick as a tome.

"You eat game?" he asks between large bites.

"Venison," I tell him, swallowing a mouthful of beef and washing it down with a fine red in a lead crystal goblet. "But this roast beef is remarkable. Never had a better piece of meat."

"Can't go wrong with roast beef," he says. "But we have some fine venison right here in our back yard. However, the best meat I ever had is Thompson gazelle roasted over an open fire. Like butter. Best meat in the world."

"What's the worst you ever had?"

"I once sat down to a meal with a tribal chief in Uganda that included human flesh," he says. "Some sort of ritualistic thing to do with a fallen enemy. Fortunately, I got wind of what was cooking, pardon the pun, and dodged that one. Told the chief I had indigestion."

The morning ride on horseback out to the aerodrome takes us through lush meadows and scattered pockets of sheep and horses to the lip of a grassy rise. Stretched out below in a shallow valley bordered by patches of forest is an airport in the making.

"There it is," Cedric says. "There's your future!"

Workers are grading the landing strip with a steam-driven bulldozer. Teams of busy technicians assemble half a dozen aeroplanes. Carpenters are building wooden structures at the head of the strip.

"Let me show you something," Cedric says, and we ride up to a new building the size of a barn. Here, the woody smell of fresh cut lumber mingles with the musky sweet scent of horses and sheep. Two men push open a large sliding door to reveal a bright red Spad. A technician's adjusting the engine. He turns, gives a thumbs up, and walks away.

"Familiar?" Cedric asks me.

"I never thought I'd see her again," I say, my heart swelling. "She looks happy in her new home."

"Care to take her up for a ride?"

"Now?"

"Of course."

"I'd like that."

"She's all yours. It's her maiden flight in England -- and yours."

When I land an hour later, Cedric is conferring with several men in suits reviewing plans on an open table. He waves me over.

"Have a look at this," he says.

Spread out on the table are architectural drawings of the finished aerodrome. It looks like a small city. He points out the various projected structures, explains their functions and how they tie together as an operating whole.

"What do you think?" he asks.

"Impressive."

"Nothing like it in the world," he ventures.

"I'd say it's a bit ambitious, considering there's nothing here that resembles these plans at the moment."

"Quite so," he says. "But growth is inevitable. The project is already funded fifty-one percent with my own money. The government will likely back some of the venture. Partners will contribute the rest. Should you choose to be one of them, I'd be happy to name you chief pilot, as well."

"The offer's tempting."

"While you think about it, I could use some help managing the project. You'll be compensated, of course. I can give you one of the cottages on the estate until you make up your mind."

"No need to wait for that," I tell him. "I knew the minute I lifted off. I'm in. We can work out all the details later."

And this is how a callow youth, jewel thief and murderer winds up a pioneer in the commercial airline business. As Cedric predicts, the blueprints become reality and private investors pour in. The fleet grows to eleven planes and after a couple of years the fleet doubles as newer models rotate in. We hire some of the world's best pilots, a few of them honored Knights of the Sky from the War. After three years my initial investment quadruples, but it never occurs to me to retire because I can't think of anything I'd rather do. In the back of my mind I toy with the idea of going back to the States and starting an air service of my own. But I'm having too much fun to think too seriously about that.

Of course, my father's initially disappointed. But when he sees how successful I am, he becomes an investor himself.

Along the way, I fall in love with Stella Fitzroy, and marry her. She's our only female pilot, a ravishingly beautiful brunette with smiling green eyes, quick wit and astonishing energy. She keeps me grounded with abundant good humor and helps me find my way when things go wrong, as they often do in new enterprises. Cedric serves as our best man, attended mostly by fellow fliers from the War dressed in full military uniform. A bevy of aristocratic nieces and in-laws throw rice and flowers as Stella and I run the gauntlet down the estate chapel steps under crossed swords.

Cedric's distant cousin, King Edward VII, and Queen Alexandra head the guest list but thankfully don't come. Instead, they send a silver tureen engraved with the royal coat of arms big enough to bathe in.

Mom and dad also fail to show up for the wedding. But soon after, my father writes to say that it had surfaced as an item in the Society Section of the New York Times.

"You're certainly flying high," he quips in a letter. "It would appear the King and Queen missed quite a show."

Actually, it was nothing of the kind. Stella and I retire to our little cottage after the wedding dinner in the main house and both dutifully report to work the next day.

I tell myself I can't possibly be any happier. Stella's lovely, delightful, full of good energy, an ideal companion for the long haul. But each time I look at the red Spad, it's inevitable that Lily comes to my mind. Then one day, the Spad's gone, sold to a collector on the Continent. But even with the Spad no longer there to remind me, I never cease wondering what had become of Lily.

I try to push her memory out of my new life. But privately I still pine shamelessly--in a way that daily bruises my conscience--for my exotic, courageous, mysterious, utterly fascinating, and ultimately unknowable Nefertiti.

The primal blood passion's still very much alive somewhere deep inside, in spite of my heartfelt efforts to make it disappear and leave me in peace.

Stella's no fool.

Maybe she can sense something.

"Do you miss her?" she asks, but not unkindly.

"Sometimes I worry about her," I confess, being totally candid. "I can't imagine why she believed she could pull off such a crazy stunt. Walking right into the lion's den. I couldn't talk her out of it. Seemed suicidal, complete destructive madness. But she was fearless, determined. I don't know what became of her..."

"From what you've told me, I'm sure you don't have to worry about Lily," she says, her voice cheerful and full of admiration.

"You'd like her," I say. "In many ways, she reminds me of you."

I should, perhaps, have worried more about Stella.

Caught in a violent storm over the Channel, she never makes it back to the field. We never find her body, nor any trace of the plane.

We'd been talking about starting a family and I'm sick with grief. She's gone and never coming back, and I realize how much my new career has robbed me of precious time I could have had with her. I feel like I've lost everything all over again. When I know I can go no lower, I make plans for a total change. I'll return to New York.

It's just then that a courier shows up with a special delivery wooden crate addressed to me.

The crate, packed with straw, contains inside it a smaller crate. Within the smaller crate is a bronze box with brass trim, latches, and a silver key on a red ribbon. Inside the box is an even smaller container, a fine red leather purse the size and heft of a fat grapefruit, stuffed tightly with what feels like gravel.

When I open the silk-lined bag, it's all I can do to remain on my feet.

In the bag is a fortune in fine-cut diamonds, sparkling wildly, as if the bag is its own source of light. I probe all the containers and attendant debris looking for a note or a return address. But the diamonds are clearly intended to speak for themselves.

After a moment I finally sit down, gawking speechless at the glittering treasure before me. I know without question Lily sent it.

Alive, and apparently well?

Has her crazy scheme somehow paid off?

If so, against all odds, how did she do it?

And why is she sending diamonds to me? What does it mean?

I hear her voice in my mind.

"I'm doing this for us."

Doing this for us.

Can I believe her? Doing this for us? How would that be? Wasn't that just an excuse to cut me loose and get on with her personal plans for power and money? Wasn't I played for a fool, just as Maurice had warned?

But still...these diamonds in my hands are real.

What message are they telling me?

Doing this for us...

The words keep repeating like a mantra. But as months pass, my excitement and curiosity cool. Eventually, I find myself thinking less and less about the diamonds and more than ever about the work at hand. I've given up all hope of ever finding Lily-- though I've tried-- or learning what has become of her, or how she could have acquired the diamonds. Or why she sent them but provided no clue as to where to find her.

The business is growing, and I must grow with it, do my part, put everything else aside and forge on.

I dive back into the daily routine with renewed zeal, spending all my days focused on growth and design.

I'm on my way to a promising career in a business I love, and if not exactly happy, at least content.

Then one bright June morning as I'm leading a potential commercial customer around the facilities, showing off our new fleet, the sun flashing off something in the sky catches my attention.

At first, I think I'm hallucinating.

A red Spad is approaching our runway. I feel the same punch in the chest you might feel running into a long-lost lover. Can this be? It can't be. I forget to breathe. No, it can't be. I watch it descend gracefully, touch down gently, and taxi across the tarmac.

The engine switches off.

This must be the new owner on a jaunt over from the Continent. Yes, that's it. Calm down.

But I know all along, from the moment I lay eyes on the red Spad in the sky, who the pilot must be.

And it is Lily who emerges from the cockpit like an impossible dream. It is Lily who jumps off the wing and turns toward me, pulling off her leather helmet, her shining raven hair cascading over her shoulders. It is Lily, a reincarnation of Nefertiti herself, radiating palpable energy I can feel even at a distance.

I'm frozen, eyes wide, without speech. I can only gaze in suspended disbelief.

She slows, then stops, facing me.

I've never seen brighter eyes, a happier face, a more beautiful smile.

We simply stare at each other, grinning.

Then, as if on cue, we rush forward. She throws herself into my arms and I hold her fast in a wondrous embrace I thought I'd never know again.

"Lily, Lily..." I finally manage, struggling to contain a whirlwind of unleashed emotion.

"Don't speak..." Her honey-smooth voice washes over me.

Several moments pass.

"I told you it would be all right..." she whispers.

In that magically transformative moment, holding her so close, I realize all over again how much she's meant to me. I know that even with the all the hurt, sorrow, betrayal, disillusionment, disappointment, shamefulness, fear and regret, I've never stopped loving her.

"The Banker...How...?"

"We shared the gift from Buffalo Bill and parted friends. The past is over." Her face is buried in my neck.

There's a long silence.

"I never thought I'd see you again," I murmur into her fragrant hair. Her scent, the feeling of her body in my arms once again, sparks renewed memories of wild passion and the deepest love I'd ever known. "I thought it was over for us ..."

"But I knew it wasn't, if you still wanted me..."

"How did you know?..."

"Because not a day went by that I didn't think of you, my love. The diamonds are for us. Freedom for us. I kept my promise..."